BRIGAND'S BLADE

Mike Liddell is a trouble-shooter for the wealthy Beauclerc family. His former partner was Roxy Barlow. After a time, a man with designs on the Beauclerc fortune exploits Roxy's weakness in liquor to gain a footing in the Beauclerc home. Roxy causes Mike some real problems — but helps fight the opposition. Madame la Baronne de Beauclerc narrowly avoids a disastrous marriage, and Mike is almost cremated before the smoke fades, in a violent and deadly showdown.

DAVID BINGLEY

BRIGAND'S BLADE

Complete and Unabridged

LINFORD
Leicester

First published in Great Britain in 1978

First Linford Edition
published 2007

British Library CIP Data

Bingley, David, *1920* –
  Brigand's blade.—Large print ed.—
Linford western library
1. Western stories
2. Large type books
I. Title II. Horsley, David, *1920* –
823.9′14 [F]

ISBN 978–1–84617–811–5 *7902074*

Published by
F. A. Thorpe (Publishing)
Anstey, Leicestershire

Set by Words & Graphics Ltd.
Anstey, Leicestershire
Printed and bound in Great Britain by
T. J. International Ltd., Padstow, Cornwall

This book is printed on acid-free paper

1

The hour was mid-afternoon in the hot season when the blue-eyed sun-bronzed rider casually steered his chestnut mount back into the main street of Sundown, Sunset County, New Mexico territory.

Mike Liddell figured he had grown used to this modest-sized town: especially in the past five or six weeks. Prior to that he had been absorbed in a critical period of risky activity in the service of the Beauclerc family whose ornate chateau was located on the north side of Sundown.

At that hour, many of the townsmen were still in the grip of siesta, but those who were awake and on the move noted the way he held himself, tall in the saddle of the muscular light brown horse. His hair was the colour of thick golden corn, long in the sideburns and at the nape of the neck.

Mike was conscious of his appearance. He knew he looked neat, as was befitting for a man in the paid service of a cultured family of titled lineage. But on the way into town centre from the chateau some three hours earlier, a drunken cowpuncher had loudly referred to him as the dude from the chateau. This appellation had hurt him. He had refrained from doing anything about it, but the taunt had rankled with him.

So much so, that as soon as he had delivered *Madame la Baronne's* white mare into the hands of the blacksmith for shoeing, he had ridden out of town to a nearby creek and there passed his time by indulging in revolver and rifle practice across the scudding waterway.

Mike was the sole surviving son of a British doctor who had served with the Confederate forces in the Civil War. Due to his late father's influence he had acquired a good education, but this had been tempered by his love of horses, and his subsequent need to make his own way in a developing west where most of the work had to do with ranching, mining and transport. He had no great love for the smell of cows, but he shared the average westerner's lack of respect for anyone who could truthfully be called a dude.

He yawned, flexed his shoulders and wondered what *Madame* would have in store for him in the way of duties when he got back. Like most men privileged to see the inside of the chateau, he was physically drawn to the beautiful French widow, and yet from time to time he tired of the modest duties which required him to be always faultlessly dressed and recently shaved.

His thoughts were elsewhere when the elderly blacksmith he had contacted earlier emerged from his shop and waved his arms urgently in Mike's direction. Here and there, men leaning on hitching posts and lounging under sidewalk awnings exchanged glances about the signalling.

Mike caught himself in the act of smoothing down his neat blue shirt, fingering his red bandanna and squaring off his new, flat-crowned fawn stetson. His voice sounded strangely harsh, as he looped a leg over his saddle horn and dropped to the dusty dirt surface of the road in front of the double-fronted establishment.

'So what's all the arm waving for, amigo?'

Jock McArthur, stooping, bald and bulky, combed perspiration from his lined brow with a hairy forearm and shrugged his thick shoulders.

'Och, I was told to hasten you, if I could, Mr. Liddell. It seems there's some sort of an emergency on at the big house. The wee laddie did not know the details, but he said *Madame* herself was mighty upset an' the Irish woman had clipped him round the ear for dawdling.'

'All right, Jock. If I'd known I'd have been back earlier. The mare is shod, all right? Good.'

Mike handed over the usual fee for all round shoeing, briefly examined the feet of the lightly built mare and remounted with a puzzled expression on his face.

★ ★ ★

The expression on the face of the elderly white-haired negro butler who opened the door showed strain. He drew Mike into the house, placed a finger to his full lips and stepped closer.

'It's *Monsieur le Comte*, Mr. Michael. He's had a heart attack. None of us below stairs know the full details. The doctor and *Madame* are with him. In his room. Miss O'Callan comes and goes. I shouldn't go up, maybe she'll come along and tell you the latest in a short while.'

Mike became aware that he was gripping the brim of his new stetson with quite unnecessary power. 'Er, all right. Thank you, Joseph.'

His feelings were mixed. This sudden

calamity had fully dispelled his feeling of boredom. Now, he thought, everything is likely to change. Mumbling that he would be in the garden, if anyone asked for him, he backed out and walked the chestnut and the frisky mare round to the stables. His mind was elsewhere as he stripped out the harness.

Presently, he found himself bareheaded again, peering down into the burial plot at the rear of the building where the remains of Dickie Beauclerc had been buried. Young Dickie had been a nephew of *Madame la Baronne*. Foul play had brought about his demise. In fact, it had been the search for Dickie, dead or alive, on Mike's part which had brought about the strong bond between young Liddell and the Beauclerc family.

He murmured: 'Well, Dickie, boy, it seems your family's troubles are about to be aggravated again. I for one don't know what will happen if the old man dies.'

Monsieur le Comte de Beauclerc was an aristocrat to his finger tips. An elderly thinned-out man with metal-rimmed spectacles, usually attired in a white suit and confined in the daytime to a wheelchair on account of a leg weakness. He was proud of his military medals and also that most of his male descendants had given their lives for France while serving in the army.

Mike was sitting on a wooden seat beside the well-tended grave when a window opened near the top of the house. The striking head and shoulders of Molly O'Callan appeared. Mike watched her, framed as she was in the window, her lush wavy red hair slightly awry and her green-eyed animated expression changed by the present emergency.

'Michael, the doctor is just leaving. *Madame* would deem it a kindness if you'd come up here now, you'll have heard the news.'

Mike was on his feet in a flash, waving acknowledgement, and starting back across the lawn. He went in this time by the back door, discarding his spurs and his hat before he raced up the secondary staircase to the upper floor.

Hearing his knock, *Madame* called him, using a curt French phrase rendered more dramatic by her emotions. She rose to her feet from beside an expensive bed with soft headboard drapes. The dark blue quilt with the family emblem worked on it was crumbled. The old man's head lay on a big French-style pillow, the mouth open as though he laboured for breath. To Mike he seemed naked without the metal-framed spectacles he wore habitually when awake.

'Ah, *Michel,*' *la Baronne* murmured, 'it has come. Finally, Papa has suffered the sort of heart attack which has threatened him for years. The doctor has just left. He has given some pills to numb any pain. The end may not come for some time. But . . . my father-in-law will never fully recover properly. He

— he will be paralysed throughout most of his body.'

Madame's voice shook as she finished her whispered revelations. Mike's eyes slewed away from the stricken old man to her, wondering just how much damage this shock had done to her. She, who had lost her husband in the service of France. Her wide-set intense blue eyes were upon his face, as though imploring him to do something, say something to comfort her.

Her shapely bosom heaved under a white peasant-type blouse, puckered at the neck. Faint freckles came and went at the base of the long neck, put there by the persistent western sun. Lower down, she had on a pair of riding jodhpurs which accentuated the shape of her hips and made her overall appearance almost irresistible.

Mike sighed. '*Madeleine*, I'm sorry.'

On most occasions, he referred to her as *Madame*, or *Madame la Baronne*, but she had permitted the use of her Christian name for a week or two, when she was sure they were not overheard. She moved into Mike's extended arms and placed her head against his chest. A seductive tremor rippled through her frame. The piled up blonde hair, giving off an odour of expensive Parisian soap or perfume, denied her forty-five years and further intoxicated her present protector.

'He can hear nothing, at the moment. What am I to do?'

'It is not for a Liddell to give advice to a Beauclerc. You must await the outcome. Other ... tragedies have matured you, shown you that you can face up to it. You are not without friends. I am wondering selfishly about myself. How can I best help in such a situation?'

Mike was aware of a change in her. 'What was the name of the undertaker, the one who provided the coffin for Dickie?'

The young Texan licked his lips and gently disengaged himself. He hesitated. 'I can't think. The shock of

Monsieur le Comte's illness has made me forget it. Why do you ask?'

Madame's troubled eyes searched his face. He had lied to her and he wondered if she knew. Earl Marden, one-time outlaw boss, did not want his name bandied about.

'I want you to seek him out, make sure he gets here with the minimum of delay. I know he comes from out of town. The undertakers in Sundown I don't care for. A burial is a special occasion in the Beauclerc family. You will find him for me, make him come straight away? Tell him no expense is spared by *la famille*.'

Under her intense, close and utterly personal survey, Mike could not refuse. He accepted this task, albeit one fraught with difficulty, as his immediate lot and devoted himself to calming the distraught woman. Amply helped by an arm, over her shoulder and under an armpit, she moved slowly out of the *Comte*'s room into the thickly-carpeted passage and on towards her own room.

11

Mike shook a small bell with his free hand, summoning a young Mexican maid, Carmelita, who was matronly-figured in spite of her modest sixteen years.

'Prepare a bath for *Madame*, and call Miss O'Callan,' he ordered.

Carmelita disappeared and was replaced by the red-haired Molly almost at once. Near the doorway of *Madame*'s bedroom the twosome paused. Mike's gaze met that of Molly, and he was aware of a certain masked hostility in the green eyes, mingled with the hurt caused by the old man's stroke.

Molly brushed back a wisp of hair, fidgeted with the frilly apron which protected her short bottle-green working dress, and took over.

'*I'll* see to *Madame* from here on in,' she remarked firmly.

Molly and Mike had known one another years earlier. The Irish woman had worked for his father over in Texas before the two of them had met again, quite by accident, in the Beauclerc household. Molly was also something of a beauty, whose looks belied her thirty-six years. At times, she was drawn physically towards this handsome fair six-footer with the stunning good looks and patrician manner, but she could not forget that she had ministered to him when he was a mere stripling boy in her earlier employment. She had sudden surges of jealousy when Mike was 'close' to her mistress.

'It would be as well, Molly,' Mike replied, keeping the tone of his voice as neutral as possible. 'However, I do have to leave, almost immediately. If I could speak to you for just a moment.'

Madame was the first to react positively. 'Yes, give Michael any help you can, Molly. I'm sending him out of town straight away.'

La Baronne half-smiled, made as if to give him a wave, then shrugged and disappeared into her room. Molly O'Callan nibbled her upper lip, and acted warily. 'Is there some difficulty, Mike?'

Lowering his voice, Mike replied. 'Yes, there is. She wants the undertaker from out of town who brought young Dickie's coffin. He's a man with secrets. Maybe he'll come, and maybe he won't.'

Molly chuckled without humour. 'Well, you have persuasive ways, even if the fellow isn't all he's supposed to be. I guess you'll need some money for expenses.'

She trotted down the staircase ahead of him and preceded him into her tiny office beside the butler's pantry. From a leather holdall in a drawer she produced a neat stack of dollar bills, some of which she separated off and gave to him, Mike nodded, smiled and hesitated.

'It won't be easy, Molly,' he admitted.

The Irish woman sighed, shrugged and suddenly raised herself on tiptoe and kissed his cheek. 'No time for food parcels, an' that will have to do for your morale.'

Moving with equal facility, Mike

grabbed her before she could back away. He kissed her warmly on the lips, and Molly — feeling a sudden quickening of interest — permitted it.

As they parted, she murmured: 'I do care what happens to you. But if you want to keep my respect you'll have the protection of this house high in your priorities. Okay? *Hasta la vista*.'

'*Hasta la vista*, Molly. Say a word to the *Comte* for me, if he recovers his faculties.'

* * *

Hard physical exercise from time to time always did Mike Liddell good. He enjoyed the punishing ride north from Sundown. His chestnut was sufficiently effective to complete a normal three hours' ride in something under two hours. A considerable quantity of dust, held in place by perspiration, had covered the dude veneer which he had become so sensitive about in and around Sundown City.

Around half past six, he was walking his mount up the centre of the main street of Sunset County's most recent settlement when the batwings of a gaudily-painted saloon on the north side of the street flew open and emitted a body. At the same time, someone in the building gave out with the finest simulated Indian war whoop he had ever heard.

The startled chestnut started to side-step round the flying body, but the ear-shattering yell was more than it could stand. Snickering fearfully, it threw up its forelegs and reared. Mike's groping gauntleted right hand narrowly missed the saddle horn, and that was the beginning of his downfall.

His butt cleared the saddle cantle and crashed into the dirt of the street not too far from a pile of animal droppings. He was shaken and angry. On hands and knees he turned towards the fellow who had been thrown out of the saloon, determined to have some satisfaction out of him, while the chestnut careered off up the street free of restraint.

The other man was a fleshy saddle tramp, breathing through his bleeding mouth and emitting the mixed fumes of beer and whisky in about equal quantities. The forehead was bony. The chest under the torn shirt was hirsute. His brown curly hair had ceased to grow on his crown.

As Mike came close to him, the other shook his head and blinked his eyes wide in an effort to clear his senses. The eyes opened still wider when they focussed on Mike.

'Mike. Mike Liddell,' the nasal voice confessed. 'Now I know I'm roaring drunk, or with the Great Spirit or something. Huh . . . '

Having said that much, the ejected drunk folded up. Out from the sensitive batwings came those who had witnessed the previous difficulties indoors. Three or four drinkers came out to jeer. They stepped aside and gave way to two others, who were angry and hatless. This pair had obviously been openly quarrelling with the fallen man.

Mike had recognised his old and worthless former riding partner, Roxy Barlow. A man he had parted company with less than two months before when he — Mike — became involved in certain tricky dealings for the Beauclercs.

While the onlookers were guffawing afresh and calling out remarks about Barlow having flattened a stranger, the two vindictive drinkers came scrambling down into the street bent on further mischief. One of them planted a boot in Mike's chest and pushed him further away, while the other one hauled up Barlow's head with his bandanna and prepared to swing a fist in his face.

Mike grabbed the offending boot, gave the ankle a vicious twist and sent its owner sprawling in the dirt. The other huge red-faced brawler hesitated, holding back his swing. Mike beckoned to him, as he rose slowly to his feet, smiling in anticipation.

'Me first, *amigo*, if you please!'

The other dropped Barlow, making an effort with his slurred speech.

'It's a pleasure, friend. Jest give me time to step over there. This, this crowbait hombre can surely wait.'

Rolling like a deep sea sailor, the big man waddled over. He poked out a long arm the better to measure the distance between himself and his intended victim. Mike ducked under it and slammed him with both fists in his ample chest. When that did not send him down a knee in the abdomen helped. The big man stepped back unsteadily. Mike followed. A blow aimed at the fellow's chin actually landed on his neck and effectually finished him as a fighting force. He went down, gasping for breath and stayed down. The other man came up in a scrambling run, catching Mike around the knees and sending him backwards. The young Texan hunched his shoulders and went down, wrestling with the other character until out of his eye corner he spied a mildewed water trough.

The supports banged across his attacker's forearms, effectively loosening his hold. Mike then thumped his opponent's big skull, almost totally visible across the crown through his thinning hair, against the trough supports. The man's eyes rolled with his senses.

Suddenly at a loose end, Mike moved wearily to his feet. A few handfuls of water from the trough helped to restore him. By a miracle he had avoided the offending animal droppings. He filled his stetson with water and poured it slowly over his old comrade's head and shoulders.

The onlookers began to see the funny side, after a pregnant silence. Mike wearily hoisted Roxy to his feet, fended off his gusty thanks and tipped a threadbare youth to go after the runaway chestnut. The barman, his ham shank arms folded over a beefy chest, looked as if he had claims against Roxy.

'If he hasn't run up too big a bill, I'll pay what he owes,' Mike offered tentatively.

'Two broken chairs, a half bottle of whisky spilled. Three or four dollars might cover it,' the barman admitted, when prompted.

Barlow's head was sufficiently clear for him to guide Mike to his room in a seedy hotel. There the veteran drifter sobered up some more and enthused over the fortuitous meeting with Mike. The latter flopped back on the bed and inhaled the smoke of a small cigar.

Encouraged by his silence, Barlow embarked upon the story of his unfortunate adventures since the two of them had parted. He had been sacked as a waddie on a ranch, thrown out of employment with a freighting company due to careless-ness with the horses, and tossed out of one rooming house because a woman complained of his amorous advances.

'Takin' it all round, it don't amount to a whole lot of wrong-doin', Mike. You know me from the old days. Well, don't you now? All I have is a few unpaid bills to take care of. Then you an' me could take up where we left off. Now, what do you say? I can see you're interested.'

'I'm interested in your line of patter, old buddy. But as for the two of us becomin' partners again, well, that's out. I'm still workin' for the Beauclerc family, an' I can't take care of you, as well.'

The absolute firmness in Mike's voice completely damped down Barlow's spirits. After a while, Roxy pressed him again. 'If you won't take me on as your pardner any more, at least give me a start. Give me something to do which takes a clear head and a steady hand. Will you do that?'

Mike found himself nodding. Roxy

then stopped pleading and waited for Mike's offer.

'I'll give you a start, for old time's sake. I'll pay all your bills, give you a small, important job to do. And that'll be it. Neither more nor less. When it's done, you drop out of circulation. You don't seek me out, and you don't try to improve upon my instructions.'

'Yer, yes, Mike. I knew you'd trust me, give me back my self respect. Tell me about it, why don't you? I won't hang around if you don't want me to.'

'If you don't act discreet in this matter, from start to finish, Roxy, you could end up dead. So could I, and so could other folks not close to the reckoning.'

This unhealthy spelling out of the possible consequences wrought a change in Barlow. Unbidden fear had suddenly dried out his mouth. He was apparently all attention as Mike talked to him, and yet his nodding seemed too automatic.

'Leave things just as they are. Get your things together. You're ridin' for Indian Ridge right away. Don't allow for any distractions. No women. And no booze. No goodbyes with other folks . . . '

2

Mike Liddell's whole frame went rigid for a few seconds as an answer to a puzzling thought broke through from his subconscious and effectively awakened him on the bed he had taken over from Roxy Barlow.

Drygulch! *That* was the name of this new settlement. And what a name for a township in the turbulent west. Mike blinked a few times, and wondered why his mind had been so troubled. The window of his room was open. A light breeze was stirring the aged curtain. Outside, and beyond the hotel, the street was relatively free of noise.

Eventually, his troubled thoughts focused on Barlow. He reflected on what had happened since his arrival in Drygulch: how Roxy had been thrust under his nose by unpredictable fate: how Roxy had been in need of help . . .

A couple of unexpected fights to keep him out of trouble. His irresponsible debts to be settled. And a chance to start afresh to be laid on for him. Mike groaned. He began to see what he had done. If he, the official bearer of tidings to Earl Marden, returned to the Chateau Beauclerc without checking on how Roxy had carried out his assignment, the whole affair might very well turn sour.

Indian Ridge, where Mike knew Earl had a contact in the newspaper office, was only a short ride from Drygulch. But clearly, several saloons would be very close to the path of his unreliable travelling companion, on the way. What if Roxy never made it to the newspaper office?

The young Texan's lips were dry. If Roxy became liquored, not only might Roxy fall down on the mission, he might commit the cardinal sin of revealing certain facts about their previous associations which were best forgotten. He sat up in bed, as the enormity of his indiscretion dawned upon him. Mike knew that Earl Marden, the undertaker, still had sufficient ruthlessness in his makeup to eliminate anyone who stood in his way, or who presented a threat to his present way of life.

Mike began to perspire. He rolled out of bed in his underwear, poured water into his hand basin and slowly bathed his face, arms and neck. He knew himself sufficiently well to realise that further sleep that night was well nigh impossible. What then?

A man's fears tended to seem greater in the dark hours. Maybe Roxy would not let him down. All the same, it would be as well to take such precautions as were still possible. It meant an immediate evacuation of the room, the hotel and the town. And ride without delay to the larger settlement of Indian Ridge. He could be there, even travelling at night by shortly after dawn. If he could be sure that Roxy had done his job, there would be no harm done.

It was not even necessary to make contact with his old comrade again.

He dried himself and began to dress. He was pleased that he had settled Roxy's debts before he turned in, and that the hotel room was paid for including that night. There was no one on duty in the livery. He checked that Roxy's horse had been withdrawn. Some ten minutes after reaching the livery stable, he had prepared his mount for the trail, and left.

★   ★   ★

The trail to the next settlement did not present any special difficulty to the horse and rider. The hour it took was long enough for Mike's mind to be assailed afresh with all sorts of doubts about his initial actions and his subsequent ones. The gentle whistling which drifted in from the east as he entered Indian Ridge had the effect of lifting his thoughts from a slight depression.

The youth who whistled was tall and skinny. He wore cut down pants, moccasins and a coarse straw hat. The wheels of the handcart he pushed needed oiling, but his facial expression was mobile enough. The track from the meadow converged with the town approach road, and he stopped whistling to grin broadly at Mike, as the latter checked his horse to speak to him.

'Good mornin', stranger. Jest goin' into town, are you?'

'Good day to you, son. Yes, I'm jest on my way in. I see you have a useful can of fresh milk on the cart. Is it for a boarding house, or maybe one of the restaurants?'

'You've guessed it, mister. My mother jest keeps enough cows in the meadow back there to see to the wants of her roomers. You wantin' a room, by any chance?'

'I could be,' Mike admitted readily enough. 'First off, though I need a bit of information, an' I don't rightly know how to get it at this hour of the mornin' without disturbin' folks.'

The youth sniffed. 'Maybe I could help.'

'I sent a buddy of mine on a message. Up from Drygulch. Last evening. Bulky fellow on a roan horse. Kind of trail soiled. Must have arrived around nine o'clock.'

'I seen him,' the youth enthused. 'Wanted to speak with Mr. Rufton, the proprietor of the *Ridge Reporter*.'

'That sounds like my friend. Do you happen to know if he made contact with Mr. Rufton?'

'He tried and failed. Mr. Rufton was out of town last evening, and his assistant wasn't around the building. One of my Ma's roomers advised him to wait until this morning. So, he acted a bit grouchy. Bedded down his roan in a Dutch barn alongside Swinson's livery, an' took a few beers. He turned in among some hay bales quite close to the hoss.'

Mike sighed, yawned and relaxed. He

thanked the youth for the information and went off with him to take a bed for what was left of the night.

★　★　★

The rooming house was clean and comfortable. Mike slept well for a few hours, having come to the conclusion that Roxy Barlow was still capable of carrying out his assignment without assistance. Towards half past eight he sauntered down to the room set aside for meals and partook of a large plateful of ham and eggs.

Around a quarter past nine, he moved out of the house and strolled up the street in search of Swinson's livery and his missing comrade. Even now, he did not plan to contact Roxy. All he wanted was to be absolutely sure that the message had been properly delivered without any embarrassing mishaps.

Jake B. Rufton, the veteran editor of the *Indian Ridge Reporter*, was sitting in his office composing an article when

Mike finally got around to the newspaper building. The young Texan stepped inside the building with a grin on his face and his stetson in his hand.

Rufton gave him a baleful look which seemed to go with the bony bronze skull topped with a white tuft of hair. The editor did not take kindly to casual customers very early in the day.

He straightened his small, cylindrical body in the creaking swivel chair. 'Something I can do for you, stranger?'

Mike paused with his booted feet apart by the end of the desk.

'Mr. Rufton, I represent a well to do family, the Beauclercs, in Sundown City. There's been an unfortunate development in the family fortunes and I had to get a message to the proprietor of the Sunset Undertaking Agency. Can you tell me if the fellow who was to bring the message has reported in?'

Rufton turned the angle of his head, eyeing him shrewdly. 'Any special reason why I should know the answer to that question?'

Mike grinned. 'I've worked with Mr. M. before. He said if he was specially wanted any time to make contact here. I'm wearing the Beauclerc ring, if you want identification. My name is Mike Liddell.'

'You checkin' up on this messenger of yours?'

'Well, yes, I found time to follow up his route. For security reasons I thought I'd make sure everything was all right.'

Rufton hesitated for a short while before telling Mike anything. The old editor felt sure that this visitor was genuine. He was pondering over the fact that Liddell did not seem to trust his own man.

'There was a message waitin' for me when I opened up this mornin'. It seems my assistant was in here earlier and he took the message from your man. In fact, he went off with your man, and I'm inclined to think he was taken along to meet the proprietor of the undertaking firm. That all you want to know, Mr. Liddell?'

Mike stuck his hat on. 'For the time being, that's all, Mr. Rufton. I take it you'll be expecting your assistant back fairly soon?'

The old man shrugged. 'It could take a little time, on account of my assistant knows Mr. M. from way back. Could be I'll have to set up most of this issue on my own.'

Mike thanked him for his time, and strolled out of the building feeling reasonably sure that little could go wrong.

★　★　★

Felix Gunther, a former road agent and member of the gang once led by Earl Marden in that same county, had taken a job as assistant to the *Ridge Reporter*'s editor, Jake Rufton, because a recent bullet wound had left him slightly incapacitated.

As recently as three months before this time, Gunther had been in the habit of taking on assignments to eliminate his fellow men. Following a confrontation with the man who set up the assassinations, he had been shot in the back. It was only the intervention of his old Boss, Earl Marden, which had enabled him to be dragged from a burning building in which his adversary had died.

In ordinary circumstances, Gunther was a twisted, vicious character who scarcely ever showed pity for any of his fellow beings, Since his 'accident' he had grown more bitter than ever. Consequently, when Roxy Barlow, a total stranger, walked boldy into the office of the Indian Ridge newspaper and confidently expected to be put in touch with the retired outlaw boss, Gunther had felt suspicious, and he was determined to sound out this bizarre character to the fullest extent of his powers before putting him in touch with Marden.

Two hours after leaving Indian Ridge, Gunther and Barlow were sharing a deserted cabin a few miles west of their starting point.

Barlow was seated at a rough hewn wooden table, sipping a large mug of coffee liberally laced with whisky. Gunther puzzled him in some ways. Roxy watched his escort as the older man paced fitfully around the worn floorboards with a belligerent frown on his swarthy, wrinkled face. He was a homely looking character, having lost most of the black hair off the front of his skull. Being slightly below the average in height, his outside muscular chest seemed really huge in his soiled blue checked shirt. A certain bulkiness amounting almost to a hunch at the back of his rounded shoulders added to the grotesque outline of his upper trunk and marked him as a man not to be trifled with.

Having circled the floor of the cabin four times, during which he had lifted his black, flat-crowned stetson as many times, Gunther paused by the window, chewing his lips and sharing his attention between his companion and his empty coffee cup.

Suddenly, he started to cough, and the cough really racked him. Barlow had no means of knowing, but this trying weakness had only assailed Gunther since he had been shot in the chest through the back.

'That sure is a bad cough you got there, Felix. Have you been to a doctor about it?'

'Aw, forget it, Barlow. It ain't nothin'.' Gunther tried to make light of his condition, but the coughing had brought the tears to his eyes, and he headed for the table and the bottle of whisky, hoping to kill the spasms which so hurt his lungs. He tipped out a few fingers into his mug and drank hard. 'The dust,' he murmured. 'Always the dust affects me.'

Barlow, who was beginning to think Gunther was employing delaying tactics instead of bringing him face to face with the undertaker, tentatively asked a question.

'Felix, you've been real good to me

since we met, but I have to ask this question. Are you expectin' the undertaker, your old friend an' comrade, to come along to this shack an' have a meeting with me?'

Having conquered his coughing fit, Gunther toyed with his whisky and moved to sit opposite Barlow, occupying the other bench.

'Well, not exactly, Roxy. Not exactly. Fact is, I have to ask you one or two questions before I take you the rest of the journey. See?'

Gunther tipped whisky into Barlow's empty mug and signed for him to drink up. The smell of it made Roxy's nostrils twitch and he did not need any second bidding. Around the time of another refill, his eyes were getting heavy and his speech slightly slurred.

'What questions, Felix, old friend?'

'About the man who sent you to Indian Ridge. Tell me about him.'

Barlow smiled at the thought of Mike Liddell. 'Mike Liddell, now there's a character for you. A man who can ride the trails with an ordinary drifter like me, an' at the same time pass for a gent with a noble French family like the Beauclerc outfit.'

Gunther cunningly looked pleased. 'How did he get involved with the Beauclercs?'

Barlow spread his calloused hands. 'That's easy, old buddy. Mike was sent by *Madame la Baronne* to look for her missin' nephew, one Dickie Beauclerc. Over in Pecos Creek, that's west of here, or south-west, I guess.'

Gunther nodded, prompting him to go on.

'He didn't find him 'cause he was dead, but he drew a bit of interest from an assassin. Fellow tried to kill my buddy, Mike, in an isolated shack with a strange name. Something Australian. Swagman's Retreat, I figure it was.'

A certain unusual harshness now crept into the voice of Gunther. For a while, Barlow, enthralled by the details of his revelations and besotted with strong whisky, did not notice.

'And your buddy, Mike. He survived, I guess?'

Barlow wiped his wet lips and nodded several times. 'He survived, all right. But something had to give. Someone had to go under.'

Roxy paused, savouring the moment for dramatically outlining the way in which Mike Liddell had bested his would-be killer. Gunther's stertorous breathing, and an unusual glint in the dark, hard eyes slowly convinced him that this protracted and seemingly innocent drinking bout might have taken a lethal turn.

3

At three o'clock in the afternoon, Roxy Barlow was in a quandary.

Shortly before midday, Gunther had appeared to grow more and more gun happy. Only the strength of the liquor which he had freely plied himself with appeared to dissuade him from using his matched hand guns on the man he was supposed to be escorting to a special meeting.

All the time Gunther had been fuming about Mike Liddell, Barlow had kept talking and hoping against hope for another change of attitude on the part of his guide. Eventually, the former assassin groaned, hiccupped a few times and reluctantly lowered his head to the table top.

The twin Colts which had earlier appeared in the fellow's hands as though by magic gradually yielded their weight to the table top. Fully a quarter of an hour elapsed before Barlow could bring himself to move. Another five minutes went by before he managed to tiptoe out of the cabin and take a few deep breaths.

There was something between this man, Felix Gunther, and the goings on of the Beauclerc family and young Mike Liddell. All Roxy's instincts told him to pull out: get clear before the bad-tempered unpredictable two-gun messenger came to his senses again and worked out what was bugging him with a session of hostile gun play.

The veteran drifter thought about it at length. He relived the earlier scenes between himself and Mike Liddell. How Mike had gradually and with much reluctance come round to the point of view that Roxy Barlow ought to be given another chance. A chance, at least, to prove that he was trustworthy as a friend.

He wondered if he ought to backtrack and try to contact Mike, but that did not seem to be feasible, inasmuch as Liddell had probably gone back from Drygulch, all the way to Sundown. There had been urgency in the way Mike explained things. The hard-to-get undertaker had to be alerted at once, and told to start for Chateau Beauclerc without delay.

If only Gunther had revealed the whereabouts of the undertaker, all would have been well. But this particular situation appeared to be a stalemate. He, Barlow, was in the hands of Gunther. Either he waited for the wild one to recover, or he mounted up and rode away from the assignment and from any remote possibility of teaming up with Mike Liddell ever again.

Gradually, faint gusts of breeze began to clear his head. He recollected that Mike had warned him to say just so much and no more. Maybe Mike already knew this Gunther by reputation. Maybe Mike would be in trouble with Gunther over what he — Barlow — had revealed already.

Still very troubled in his mind, he walked slowly away from the isolated cabin in the direction of the sound of moving water. Some two hundred yards away, he came upon a stream. One of the reasons, no doubt, why the original cabin builder had settled where he did.

Roxy sat himself down and smoked. The gentle sounds of the water ripples soothed him a little. He set his head and shoulders between forking tree roots, pushed his hat over his face and easily slipped off into sleep.

About three in the afternoon, he began to wake up again. Whenever he could he took a short siesta, and over the years three p.m. was a significant time for him. He sat up and looked around. No sign of activity from the direction of the cabin. The thin plume of smoke which had earlier graced the cloudless sky seemed to have faded away. Even the horses had strayed over a low mound, cropping grass out of sight.

It was borne in upon Roxy that he

was far from clean. He never spent any significant amount of money on soap, and here was an opportunity to remove from himself some of the dirt, grime and perspiration which more or less marked him down as a permanent trail person.

He rose to his feet, yawned, discarded his stetson and began to strip off his shirt. A minute or two later, naked, he moved cautiously into the shallows, marvelling at the paleness of his skin where his clothes normally covered it.

Branches, mosses and mud at the bottom were soon forgotten. He pushed off, blowing water out of his face, and soon he was swimming backwards and forwards with cumbersome but effective strokes and remembering episodes from his childhood when his folks had lived in terrain such as this.

The first gun-shot startled him, but not as much as it might have done on account of his ears being below the surface of the water. The brief pale furrow which was the path of the second bullet passed through the water an inch or two above his bare back and at once alerted him to the fact that someone was shooting at him.

It needed no brain work to figure that Gunther had recovered, and that he was still in a mood for lethal or semi-lethal tricks . . .

Roxy turned towards his tormentor. 'Hey, Felix, turn it in, will you? A guy could get hurt! It ain't safe, shootin' at water!'

As a result of the protest, Gunther stepped out into the open, one long-barrelled gun in each hand. He was grinning like a man with no teeth and getting a great kick out of tormenting the defenceless swimmer.

At the same time, Barlow was almost sick with fear. He felt reasonably certain that if he tried to swim away he could wind up with a bullet in his head. Gunther, he figured, was not quite as mentally fit as he ought to be. The only alternative was to face up to him, brazen it out. He thought fleetingly that maybe he wasn't ever going to be any good without Mike Liddell around to back him and protect him.

'I'm comin' out! I've got business to transact, remember?'

Gunther brought up his weapons, moving them with precision. He squeezed both triggers at exactly the same time and sent two bullets on a slightly descending trajectory under the advancing swimmer.

Barlow gasped, coughed water out of his mouth, hastily filled his lungs and dived. He was not much good at surface-diving but any man will try when threatened on the surface with firing guns.

He swam until his lungs protested and bright lights formed behind his eyes. Then he came up. On the way he turned onto his back, and later he hung on the surface like a dying fish, belly uppermost and oblivious to the continued shooting.

Eventually, Gunther gave up, on

account of his guns being empty, and Barlow was able to stagger clear unmolested. The latter moved as far as his clothes and began to roughly dry himself and dress. Gunther now ignored him, thumbing shells into his weapons and lovingly fingering the moving parts which had been oiled the day before.

Barlow decided to try a bluff. 'I don't know what your aim is in life, Felix, but I'm through with you. Maybe I got the wrong man when I went to the *Reporter* office. I wouldn't know. All I do know is that the message I was supposed to deliver was urgent. Undertakin' ain't no sort of a business for fools. I was takin' a genuine request from folks who ain't used to bein' let down.

'It's my belief that the undertaker ought to hear what I have to say. If he doesn't like me, or objects in any way, he can speak for himself. There's been too much delay already. So, if you ain't liquored up no more, maybe you'll tell me where to find him, or lead the way.'

Roxy was about to add that perhaps a swim in fresh cool water might help, but he thought better of it and simply awaited some reaction from the listener. Gunther was in no hurry to answer. Barlow waited without complaining. He dressed, pulled on his boots and began to feel uncommonly warm again.

Still no reaction from Gunther who remained seated with his legs forked apart. Gunther allowed a gap to develop between them. While they were still pacing their way back to the shack, another development was fast approaching.

★ ★ ★

Mike Liddell had been acting with almost as much uncertainty as his old riding partner since their most recent meeting. Shortly after noon he had returned to the newspaper offices on a hastily thought-up pretext and he had cajoled a wary Jake Rufton into telling him exactly where the undertaker was to be found.

As it happened, the remote cabin where the devious Gunther had taken Roxy Barlow was directly en route for Marden's country hideout, a former relay station. Purely by chance, therefore, Mike was within hearing distance of the narrow swimming creek when Gunther loosed off the bullets to harass the balding swimmer.

Instinct more than anything else made him turn off the ill-defined trail in the direction of the shooting. His senses were fully on the alert when the ears of the chestnut horse shifted a few degrees and he became aware of the familiar roan horse cropping grass with a slackened saddle swaying gently on its back.

He loosened his Winchester in the saddle scabbard and prepared for the worst. In remote draws, a man had to be prepared to look after himself. Slowing his mount, he vaulted to the ground and catfooted towards the roan in order to double check it. It was Roxy's, all right.

Roxy and gun shots. That could mean anything, except that Roxy was not in the habit of taking time out between stops to indulge in target practice. Nor was he supposed to be alone. He was supposed to be in the company of a man well known to Earl Marden. And this, clearly, was not the location of the old relay station where Marden and his boys had gone to earth.

Mike pushed the chestnut in the direction of the roan and ran forward to the nearest of the screening trees. The sight that met his eyes gave him food for thought. Roxy was no more than fifty yards away. The man who followed him was about a similar distance further away, and toying with twin Colts which he spun occasionally by the trigger guards.

Roxy had his hat on the back of his head, and he was carrying his gun belt and vest rather gingerly. His sparse hair suggested that he had been in the creek.

Clearly, there was tension between the two approaching men. They were headed for a shack now quite visible beyond the trees.

Mike licked his lips and began to weigh up the situation. It appeared that for once Roxy was in difficulty from no fault of his own. A cooling of the present situation might reveal that he had talked too much, but this far Mike had to give him the benefit of the doubt.

Anyway, Roxy had not clashed with Marden, nor with any of the ex-outlaw's known assistants. This man with the business-like guns, he was familiar, but not on account of his being with Earl. Checking his hand reflexes, Mike knew he had to do something before the walkers reached the shack. As soon as they were inside, Roxy could be beyond help for a short while.

He found a rest for the barrel of his Winchester on a low tree branch, made himself reasonably comfortable, and cleared his throat.

'Howdy, gents! I'd take it as real friendly if you'd stop right where you are an' face this way!'

His voice had a startling effect. Roxy jumped an inch or so in the air and dropped the items he was carrying. Gunther leapt as though he had been stung, and quickly faced the direction of the threat with his twin guns held at the ready, but wavering, not knowing the exact location of the spoken menace. As Mike coughed, Roxy sighed with relief and began to collect his vest and belt from the ground.

'Shucks, Mike, you sure did give me a turn. But I'm real glad you happened along right when you did.'

'Is that mean lookin' hombre botherin' you at all, Roxy? It was gun shots attracted me this away.'

Barlow sniffed. 'Well, it was him that fired the shots. Trouble is, I can't tell when he's foolin' or when he's drunk. I'd have taken the message to the undertaker long before now if Felix hadn't stopped here an' made a fool of me. Honest, Mike, that's the gospel truth.'

Mike answered: 'Yer, Felix, you're kind of makin' me nervous. Why don't you holster those guns an' keep them that way? I'm the man who wants Earl Marden, and Rufton told me exactly where to find him. So don't go playin' any tricks on me.'

Gunther let out his breath in a long quiet whistle. The unwinking muzzle of the Winchester made him holster his guns against his own inclinations.

'All right, mister, come on up to the cabin. I won't do anything unfriendly until we've talked, an' that's a promise.'

Gunther then took the initiative, heading Barlow into the cabin and topping up the coffee pot once again. Roxy and Mike came in with a short interval between them, both fully on the alert. To further ease the situation, Gunther had hung up his gun belt on a hook.

The former assassin took to pacing

again. Mike explained how their paths had crossed in the Wampum bar, Indian Ridge, a few weeks ago. On that occasion, Gunther had quit the bar rather pointedly before Mike could offer him a drink. Ignoring young Liddell's softening-up talk, the restless one embarked upon an explanation.

'I've known Earl Marden a long time, young fellow. In fact, I owe my life to him, from the time of the fire, in Indian Ridge.'

'I was in the Sternfeld emporium at the time of the fire,' Mike remarked conversationally. 'But I didn't see you there. In fact, it was Sternfeld himself I dragged out. Already dead. Shot.'

Gunther stopped pacing and coughed. For a brief second or two his eyes opened really wide. Surprise transformed his face.

'If you're thinkin' I shot Sternfeld, you're mistaken. He shot me. Earl pulled me out. You must have arrived later. In any case, the details don't matter none now. In bringin' your buddy, Barlow, here, I was protectin' Earl from a man who might be settin' him up. That's all. Mind you, in admittin' this, I ain't sayin' you're above suspicion.'

Roxy clumsily poured the coffee, splashing Mike's hand. The Texan winced, but said nothing. His attention was still with Gunther.

'Why should I be under suspicion, just because I want to get in touch with Earl? After all, we *have* worked together recently. That must count for something. We parted on good terms in Sundown, not so very long ago.'

Gunther shrugged, and seated himself on the lower of two bunks, not far from where his gun belt was hanging. He chuckled, without humour.

'Uh huh. But Earl, as you may know, is a man who takes care of his own private business. I wonder, for instance, if he knows you are the man who killed his only brother, Ringo. You are a man who looks sort of determined to me. You might have taken on a secret job to kill both the Marden brothers. Bein' suspicious of strangers often prolongs a western man's life, wouldn't you say?'

Mike sighed. 'I think you must have been pickin' my partner's brains. Maybe it wasn't a wise thing to do, askin' him to contact a known outlaw keen to keep his new identity secret. I *did* kill Ringo. It was the only way to stay alive. I was askin' questions on behalf of the family I'm workin' for now. Earl was bound to find out about how Ringo died, sooner or later.

'In any case, I still have to contact Earl. He's worked for the Beauclercs already, and I'm sure we can work out our differences without any hostile gun play. So when do we start?'

'You sound plausible enough, young fellow,' Gunther admitted, through the steam from the coffee. 'But I still have doubts.'

Something in Gunther's attitude needled Mike, who said: 'You seem well informed about Ringo. Have *you* ever been employed to kill anyone?'

Somehow, Gunther's gun belt had

reappeared round his middle. Now, he reacted quickly. As one, he and Mike rose to their feet. Mike's right hand and both of Gunther's hovered in the air, prior to a quick draw. A second or two passed.

Barlow said: 'Why don't you two gents postpone showin' your intense dislike for each other till we get to the undertaker's place? I'm sure Mr. Marden will think his business is important enough not to have the meetin' delayed indefinitely.'

Roxy sounded calm enough, but twin trickles of perspiration which had nothing to do with the coffee were coursing down his face.

His suggestion was accepted.

4

Earl Marden's remote headquarters were perhaps another quarter of an hour's ride in a westerly direction. There was a little friction on the way, concerning who should lead and who should be permitted to follow. So that neither Felix nor Mike should have to show his back to the other, this pair agreed reluctantly to ride along side by side.

Roxy Barlow, with his head full of conflicting thoughts, brought up the rear.

The Marden outfit was spread over two or three acres. It comprised a big solid-looking ranch house with a useful turret on the roof for distant observation, a small blacksmith's shop, a hut which had once served as a bunkhouse, and two stables. Flanking it were two sizeable corrals and a barn which now functioned as a coach house for two hearses and other light vehicles.

Barlow drew level with the other two as the horses speeded up on the run in. It was noticeable that Gunther became less vigilant. Mike interpreted this as a sign that others would be on the lookout.

A gentle monotonous tapping stopped in the smithy as a veteran Mexican heard the sounds of approaching hooves. By the side of the house, Rusty Bayer straightened up behind the pump. All three newcomers could see that he was tense, and it became apparent when he recognised Gunther and Mike Liddell that he was holding a rifle alongside the pump handle.

Rusty's tight thin mouth manoeuvred into what passed for a smile. He nodded, whistled for the benefit of other alert watchers, and sauntered forward to greet the new arrivals. Up in the turret, used at one time as a lookout post for marauding Indians, Sam Bayer, Rusty's younger auburn-haired brother, whistled an acknowledgement. His grin was also something of a failure on account of his nose having been flattened in early manhood by an outsize fist.

'Howdy, boys,' Gunther yelled, 'I've brought this here fellow along to see the Boss, on account of he says he knows you all. I reckon you do, otherwise you wouldn't be so pleased to see us.'

'We know him, sure enough, Felix,' Rusty acknowledged, as he came close. 'He's a good hand with a shovel, an' other less weighty tools. Come on inside, why don't you? Earl is sunnin' himself on the back gallery. I reckon it's about time to pack up work for the day. I'll join you in just a minute.'

Swallowing his distaste for Mike, Felix headed the other two into the mellow wooden house, and furtively tiptoed into the best room with his spurs doing a quiet tune and his broad-rimmed hat suffering in his nervous fingers.

Mike gestured for Roxy to take a

seat, while he himself found his way through to the rear, and politely coughed to alert the formidable-looking fellow behind the newspaper in the creaking rocking chair.

'Mr. Marden, I'm sorry to intrude upon your privacy. I was sent here by *Madame la Baronne de Beauclerc*. She was pleased about the way you handled the other business, to do with puttin' her nephew in the casket an' she insisted on my contactin' you for another job.'

Marden lowered the paper sufficiently far to take a sharp look at his visitor over the top of it. As Mike explained the reason for his visit, the former gang leader relaxed, threw away the paper, and gestured for Mike to take one of the vacant wicker seats.

'Good to see you again, Liddell. Make yourself comfortable. Did you have any trouble gettin' here?'

From a seated position, Mike replied: 'Not really. As a matter of fact I entrusted the actual contact to an old buddy of mine. Perhaps it wasn't such a good idea. I got to thinkin' that afterwards, so I followed him up to make sure he'd contacted your agent in Indian Ridge an' not done anything foolish.'

As Mike paused, Marden prompted him. 'And did he?'

'I can't rightly be sure. However, he made contact with your man, Felix, who took him off-trail a mile or two back and started to pump bullets at him. I don't want to complain, but I think Felix overdid the business of protectin' you. He's unpredictable to say the least. And if it hadn't been for the bullets I have a feelin' Roxy might never have got here with the message. I mean I wouldn't have known where to look to protect him from Felix. If you see what I mean.'

Marden nodded curtly and withdrew into himself. The rocker stopped moving. Mike felt free to observe him. He was a tall, lean, muscular man in his forties with a Roman nose set in a cleanshaven face like tanned leather. His sandy hair was short with silver highlights in it. One grey sideburn was slightly longer than the other.

'Let's go through,' Marden decided, rising smoothly and quickly to his feet.

Mike also stood up. He stepped aside and followed his host through to the sitting room where Felix hovered nervously and Roxy slouched in a chair. The mere presence of the old outlaw had the effect of pinning the attention of the ill-assorted couple. Mike indicated Roxy and named him, and all four seated themselves afresh. Marden's chair was behind a table: the other three used upright chairs across from him.

'Felix, how come you thought it was necessary to come along here with Liddell's messenger?'

Suddenly, Gunther was bereft of his domineering role. He gripped his knees through his denim trousers and worked hard not to wheeze or cough.

'Shucks, Boss, I was only seekin' to protect you.'

'Rufton had orders to co-operate with Liddell, if he ever showed up. Rufton is reliable. I think you took a lot on yourself.'

Marden undid another button on his checkered shirt. He was breathing more deeply than he had been.

'This — this fellow Liddell sent along didn't appear to be all that reliable to me, Boss. I'm sorry if I overdid it. I got to thinkin' when Barlow talked that maybe your contact Liddell wasn't as reliable as he made out.'

Marden sniffed. 'Why?'

Gunther started to gesture with his hands. 'Well, he seems to know a lot about Sternfeld and the fire. Claims to have dragged Sternfeld out by himself.

'All that I know,' Marden replied coldly. 'If I hadn't dragged you out, maybe Liddell might have been the one to save you. What else is troublin' you, Felix?'

Gunther fought down an urge to

start coughing, but his breathing had become noisy. 'Then did you know that Liddell was the one to shoot your brother, Ringo, in an isolated cabin known as Swagman's Retreat?'

For a short while, there was no sound within the room. Everyday sounds from out-of-doors seemed magnified through the open window. Presently, Gunther stopped holding his breath, and Barlow, who had turned a pallid grey colour, slumped in his seat. Somehow, due to his brain being fuddled, Roxy had not understood the connection between this veteran ex-outlaw leader and the assassin Mike had despatched at an earlier date.

Mike found the tension building up in himself. Marden's fingers were linked so that his knuckles stood out like white knobs and the veins protruded on the backs of his hands.

'Earl, I'm sorry the way that encounter turned out, but only for your sake. I couldn't do any other. I knew you'd find out one day, sooner or later.

Apologies don't do any good, so I won't labour the point.'

The silence grew again. One Bayer brother appeared in the doorway, and then the other. Aware of the tension in the room, they catfooted forward and took seats near the window, away from the rest. Rusty Bayer's knee joint creaked. Earl Marden glanced across at him.

'I knew how Ringo died weeks ago. My sources of information in and around Pecos have always been good. It tears me apart to have to behave well with the man who killed my brother, even though the violence was thrust upon him.'

'I knew how you felt, Earl,' Gunther put in. 'I guess I was right.'

Suddenly Earl parted his hands and pointed a horny finger in Gunther's direction. 'If you know me so well, you'll also know how I feel about the ornery galoot who introduced my brother to the assassin business. If you hadn't shown him the way, Felix, he would have been alive and well and probably sittin' beside me right now.'

Gunther wanted to express his sorrow but he was deprived of words due to the tension in him and the chest weakness which was a legacy of his most recent wound. His laboured breathing, and a cough which seriously threatened his equilibrium, drew the attention of all towards him.

There was no compassion in Marden's voice, even so. 'Felix, I want you to stay with Rufton an' become a good assistant to him. Don't interfere with my business in future. If I want you, I'll send for you. Is that understood?'

Gunther rose to his feet, still breathing heavily and nodding in a way which would have strained his neck, in time.

'Now, get yourself back to town, an' keep out of trouble!'

No one moved until the humiliated man had left the building and mounted his horse. Only then did Marden relax sufficiently to call for a bottle of whisky, and to ask why the Beauclercs wanted the services of an undertaker after so short an interval.

★ ★ ★

Around midnight, the whisky was consumed, Rusty Bayer and Barlow retired first, neither having done very well in the poker game which passed the time after the evening meal. Sam Bayer went next, and Mike found himself stretched out in an easy chair, sharing the dying embers of a wood fire in Earl Marden's company.

Earl shifted a gnarled pipe stem around to the side of his mouth, and regarded his guest through hard eyes shaded by sun-bleached brows.

'I'm glad you came. The only weakness I see in my defences, as a result of your visit, is in the character of your buddy, Barlow. In fact, I think you must have doubted him yourself, otherwise you wouldn't have followed him.'

69

Mike nodded, removed his short cigar to reply, but Marden was not finished. The older man buttoned up his waistcoat, as though a slight drop in temperature was affecting him.

'Me an' my boys, the Bayers, will be leavin' for Sundown shortly after breakfast in the mornin'. We ain't short of funds, an' I don't mind bein' away for a while. Folks who want us and don't make contact usually save themselves cash by doin' their own funeral arrangements.

'Now, about Barlow. What do you have in mind?'

Mike sighed. 'He is unreliable, otherwise I might still be ridin' the trails with him instead of doin' jobs for *la Baronne*. I shall leave with him at a different time, take him in another direction an' do all I can to have him permanently distracted and removed from the district. Apart from counselling him about havin' a loose tongue.'

Very slowly, Earl Marden relaxed. 'You've acquired quite a lot of wisdom for a young fellow still in his middle twenties, Mike. I bet you're all the rage with *Madame* an' some of them fancy ballroom women!'

Mike had the grace to blush. Suddenly he turned serious. So much so that Marden stiffened up a bit.

'Sorry if I startled you, Mr. Marden. I was just thinkin'. Before I took up with him, Roxy was mighty keen on female company. I think you've just given me a good idea how to handle him.'

The pair were still chuckling when an expensive clock chimed. Earl yawned, and intimated that it was time for them both to retire.

* * *

Around eight p.m. the following evening, Mike Liddell and Roxy Barlow rode into the recently-established township of Eastville, which was ten miles nearer Texas than Drygulch, the settlement where the two had renewed their acquaintance.

During the early part of the day, they

had shared the journey with Earl Marden and his boys who were headed for Sundown and taking short cuts. The undertaking outfit had avoided Indian Ridge, which had pleased Mike, and the riders had only parted from the hearse's crew when the secondary trail they were using crossed the regular Indian Ridge-Sundown City track.

Barlow had started the day in a carefree, light-hearted fashion. His spirits were even higher when the time to separate from the Marden crew came around. The parting with Barlow was rather cool on the part of the Marden trio, but Roxy did not appear to notice.

It was only when Mike indicated that he had no intention of entering Drygulch that Roxy began to realise that there were strings attached to his recent deliverance from trouble. The veteran drifter became introspective, then he sniffed and coughed, and finally asked questions.

'So what sort of deal did you do with Earl Marden on account of me?'

Mike was slow in answering. 'I had to guarantee that your lips would stay sealed on certain topics, an' that your trail would never cross Earl Marden's again. That's why we're headin' more or less in the direction o' Texas, old buddy.'

Roxy gave his roan a touch of the rowel. 'You're takin' what Marden says real serious, ain't you, old friend?'

Mike nodded. 'Otherwise, he might have you shot.'

This blunt utterance had the effect of killing conversation until the run-in to Eastville. Both riders were tired, thirsty and far from their best. They rode up the central thoroughfare without enthusiasm until Barlow spotted a peeling entertainment notice outside a big saloon with a picture on it suggesting that *Mademoiselle* Marie-Louise would be performing in the Uncle Sam saloon for an indefinite period.

Roxy, who did not read well, stared at the picture of the buxom female entertainer in fishnet tights, sitting on a trapeze and showing a lot of provocative curves. At once, his heavy brow cleared. His mouth spread into a big smile, and he leaned out of the saddle to slap Mike across the chest with the back of his gloved hand.

'Old friend, I don't think you're goin' to have to worry about my future any more. That there girl on the trapeze is none other than my old sweetheart, the celebrity singer an' dancer, Miss Melindy-Lou! Will you believe that?'

Mike did not even think about Melindy-Lou of Roxy's memories having anything to do with this Marie-Louise. All he could think of was further involvement, further trouble on his old partner's behalf. He wondered how much more time he could afford to waste before hurrying back to the Beauclerc base in Sundown City.

5

The township of Eastville had few quiet hours between the heat of one day and the next. Sarcastic visitors often suggested that the drunks kept the settlement ticking over when the God-fearing were trying to sleep. Others suggested that something special was added to the beer and whisky which had the effect of making raucous singers out of the quietest and mildest of men.

Around two o'clock in the morning after Barlow and Liddell had arrived, the town marshal was dozing in a chair with his boots resting on top of the stove in his office due to an unexpected lull in the turnover of drunks.

The formidable Uncle Sam saloon enjoyed a boom in custom during the hours between nine and midnight, but since the witching hour everything had gone silent. The beer-swilling pianist had passed out. The night barman had stretched out on his mattress in his makeshift cellar behind the bar, and those who had fallen asleep earlier among the tables had dragged themselves away to a more comfortable place for rest.

Here and there, a turned-down lamp dimly illuminated the soiled features of the main room, which was two storeys high. On the ground floor, the long bar spanned one side. Gambling tables occupied most of the side opposite. Facing a new arrival in the far wall was the shallow stage. The claret draw curtains were in place, masking the backcloth decor and the swinging trapeze from which the celebrated *Mademoiselle* Marie-Louise did her main 'stunt' of the evening.

Shortly after two a.m., one of the doors opening out onto the balcony quietly opened and a scantily clad female figure emerged without haste and leaned over the banisters, looking down into the great well of the public room. She had closed the bedroom door behind her, and was humming a popular tune to herself, although her mouth was not empty.

In fact, she was smoking a small dark cigar which she had acquired during the evening from an inebriated visitor who insisted on giving her something. She had on dancing pumps, which she always favoured instead of slippers. Her hour glass figure, her generous bosom and strong shapely legs were clad only in a diaphanous pale blue nightdress, over which she had slung a man's military cloak of dark blue cloth piped around the edges with scarlet.

In one hand, she carried a thin-stemmed wine glass half full of champagne. In the other was a small neat lamp. Still humming to herself and still encumbered, she danced a light waltz along the length of the narrow balcony giving access to the rooms.

Presently, she tired of the exercise. Instead, she moved down half of the stairs to the turn. There, she put down her lamp, turned up the wick and seated herself, stretching luxuriantly and sighing with pure satisfaction. She stared at the champagne almost unblinkingly for a time, and then drank it, swallowing only once.

In the daytime, her shoulder length dark brown hair was usually piled and pinned on the top of her head. Now, it was released, and it cascaded loosely framing her features in shadow with its becoming brown bell.

A man's footsteps echoed faintly along the sidewalk boards, pausing briefly and then stepping inside the batwings, which swung and creaked, slowly diminishing in volume and movement.

The newcomer was tall and lean: perhaps thirty-five years old, with a latin cast of feature. His thick black hair was brushed straight back from the forehead under the flat-crowned stiff-brimmed type of hat favoured by a bull-fighter. The thin bow of moustache was trimmed back so that only a few millimetres stood clear of the upper lip. The sideburns were short. A tapering Grecian nose with mobile nostrils separated a pair of hard blue eyes. The lean sliver of scar tissue above the angle of the left side of the jaw was in shadow. The pointed chin had a cleft. Long spatulate fingers drummed lightly on the front of his black vest, which was worn loosely over a neat white shirt and a string tie. A twin gun belt of light-coloured leather contrasted in colour with his tight-fitting, tailored black trousers.

He said softly: '*Tu es la*, Marie-Louise?'

She removed the cigar from her lips and glanced in the direction of the newcomer, showing no marked interest.

'Yes, I am here, Ramon. May I ask where you have been?'

Ramon stilled his fingers and made an effort to refrain from flaring his nostrils. Eventually, he managed a deep-throated chuckle.

'*Ma cherie*, I have to admire your

nerve. Whether you are calling yourself Marie-Louise, or Melindy-Lou, or even your real name — '

'My real name is Manuela Sanchez,' the girl on the stairs put in, 'and I don't tell that to many people, Ramon. Consider yourself honoured.'

The Frenchman sniffed and slowly walked through the drinking area to the foot of the stairs. 'I was about to say that you never lose your cool, even when you have placed yourself in a position of some danger.'

He placed one shiny boot on the lowest step, and stared up at her. He acted as if his eyesight took in everything, in spite of the semi-gloom.

'Me, I have been on the town. As for you, you have had a busy evening. When I left, the drunks were clamouring around the catwalk as if they would pull you down amongst them. The sight of you in fishnet tights does things to their unimaginative drink-sodden minds.

'I was particularly interested in the drunken saddle drifter. The one who stood on the bar and yelled one of your other names at you. Melindy Lou. When he made a paper dart, folded a dollar bill around it and launched it at you, you caught it.'

Marie-Louise rubbed out her cigar butt on the stairs and dropped it through the banisters. 'You think this saddle drifter is interesting enough to take your place in my affections?'

She examined her nails in the light of the lamp, while the tormented man down below had a battle with his rising temper.

'Don't trifle with me, *mademoiselle*,' he murmured menacingly. 'A friend told me he was taken away to your private room. What do you say to that?'

Marie-Louise yawned. She had a passion for taunting men which bordered on lunacy. 'I say your friend was well informed. Roxy Barlow is in my room. I can't deny it.'

The narrow-bladed throwing knife which had been secreted at the back of Ramon's waistbelt was betrayed briefly as lamplight caught the reflecting quality of the business end. It stuck in the handrail above Marie-Louise's head and quivered there. Although she was shaken the girl merely shuddered and retained her control.

'Oh, Ramon, you were always a little theatrical in your gestures. I know your lethal qualities already. There was no need to demonstrate with your knife.'

He was coming up towards her, moving lightly, two steps at a time. For her, the temperature seemed to have dropped. Under the enveloping military cloak she shuddered.

'As I move nearer, I wonder if there is any reason why I shouldn't slit your throat in this hell house where you flaunt yourself!'

Moving her legs together and shuffling a little nearer the rails, Marie-Louise dipped into a pocket of the cloak and produced a roll of dollar bills. Ramon towered over her, a hand resting on the handle of the dagger, prior to hauling it out of the woodwork.

He murmured: 'You have taken money from this — this Roxy Barlow? Is that what you are saying?'

'I don't have to take money from Roxy. He has wanted to marry me for quite a long time. He could be a threat to you, if I wanted a husband.'

'You come out here, dressed like that, using my military cloak, at a time when you are, what shall we say? entertaining that no account drifter. I'll tell you what I'll do. I will go and slit his throat. On your bed!'

He yanked the dagger out of the woodwork and ran up the remaining steps, revealing his extreme fitness, even at that hour of the morning.

'Ramon! Wait!'

He crossed the narrow balcony and only paused when he had his hand on the knob of her bedroom door.

'If you have a reason for stopping me, it will have to be a good one, because I don't have the same patience at this hour of the night. Besides, I think our relationship has reached a stage when you need to be taught a lesson. I think the time is ripe.'

She murmured: 'The Chateau Beauclerc.'

'What did you say?'

'There is a connection between this man, Roxy Barlow, and the Chateau Beauclerc. Come and sit by me. I will tell you about it.'

Considerably intrigued, the hot-blooded would-be assassin went back to the stair and gave his full attention to his *amour* of the moment.

'Barlow came to town with an old friend. A man called Mike Liddell. Liddell actually works for *Madame la Baronne*. What do you think of that?'

Ramon whistled. 'So, a connection, at last. This Barlow, he is reliable? He was not making up this story of the connection?'

'Roxy is anything but reliable, but he did not make up the story. I know this because his friend, Mike, came to see me. Mike paid me ten dollars to resume my relationship with Roxy. It seems Barlow is not wanted near the chateau.

And there are others, with secrets, who fear his tongue. I entered into a word of mouth bargain to help Roxy on his way over the Texas border when he gets restless again. Now, what do you think of that?'

Shaking with enthusiastic, silent laughter Ramon slipped under the military cloak and snaked an arm round Marie-Louise. She folded herself against him, chuckling at his sudden change of mood.

He said into her ear: 'And your friend, Roxy, he confirmed what the other one had said?'

'Oh, yes, he would tell me anything, especially when he's liquored. He said his old buddy, Mike, once broke into the chateau for a dare. Now, he has gone all respectable, and *Madame's* obedient servant.'

'Do you think Liddell would help me?'

'No, he's more interested in my sort of intrigue than yours. You'll have to make use of Roxy and leave the other

85

one out of the reckoning.' She yawned. 'I say, aren't you tired? What are we doing here?'

Ramon grunted. He carefully picked her up and carried her to the nearest of the unoccupied rooms.

★ ★ ★

Roxy met the dashing Ramon over breakfast some time after nine a.m. the following morning in a stylish restaurant run by a couple of Italians. Ramon pretended more than a passing interest in Roxy, and paid his food bill before taking him off to see the sights of the modest town.

About eleven, they had their first session of cards with a travelling man and an infrequent visitor. Roxy appeared to do well, and he won a few dollars. Around the hour of noon, Ramon went away on an errand and a sly secretive fellow came up to Roxy and informed him that his seemingly amiable companion had another side to his nature. Less than a week earlier, he had shot a fellow card player through the heart with a small Derringer pistol, for cheating.

This revelation jolted Roxy, who had earlier been told by Marie-Louise that Ramon had been her lover, and that he was of a very jealous nature. So far, it seemed, Ramon did not know who spent the night — or part of it — with her.

In the afternoon, Roxy lost a few dollars at cards. He and Ramon then drank a lot of whisky and duly passed out for a siesta. It was during the noisy evening session in the smoke-ridden overcrowded Uncle Sam saloon that Barlow began to lose rather seriously.

At first, Ramon laughed at him, and jokingly suggested that he was losing on purpose to accommodate a friend. Ramon encouraged him to speculate more and more and more, until Roxy was nearly four hundred dollars out of pocket and his partner had to pay off the other players.

Ramon then left him, and warned him to stay where he was and keep off the cards. The Frenchman returned to the saloon as the seasoned drinkers were thinning out.

'*Mon ami*, you are in trouble. You owe me money, nearly four hundred dollars, and you have attempted to come between my intended and myself. In my family we believe in swift justice. The duel. What would you prefer? The pistol, the knife? Name your weapon.'

Roxy's ravaged face and bloodshot eyes did not show up well, as he cowered over the saloon table. 'Believe me, Ramon, when I came here, I had no intention of interfering in your life in any way. All I wanted was a little fun. If, if there was some other way I could make it up to you. Not duelling, That's not my line . . . '

'There is one way, *mon ami*.'

'Name it,' Roxy begged him, while he patiently lighted a fresh cigar.

'You will take me to the Chateau Beauclerc, soon. Perhaps tomorrow.

And when we get there, you will do me a favour. A big favour. Then, and only then, will all debts between you and me be settled. What do you think?'

Ramon appeared to turn his attention away from the distressed man while he went through the motions of manicuring his nails with his favourite throwing knife. From time to time, he glanced up, and eyed his victim keenly. Warring fears and doubts made a playground of turmoil in Roxy's face.

Ramon murmured: 'Maybe the duel is less irksome?'

'Oh, no. No. There will be difficulties at the Chateau Beauclerc. Particularly as I have been warned to stay away. But if that is the only alternative, I will try to help you, Ramon.'

Ramon appeared to unwind. He handed over two silver dollars, and told Roxy to go and enjoy himself in another building. Some ten minutes earlier, Marie-Louise had gone off up the stairway to her room. The discomfited drifter knew without telling that he would never mount that staircase to her room again.

He left the building with his thoughts in a state of depression.

6

In Sundown City, the veteran stricken *Comte de Beauclerc* lingered on. His illness, which was expected to prove fatal by all who knew his condition, obviously affected those who loved him and the regular working staff of the chateau.

Madame la Baronne had withdrawn into herself, given up horse-riding for a time, and left most of the decision making to Molly O'Callan. The latter, being capable and most scrupulously honest, carried the burden of responsibility without demur, and yet she suffered, too, on account of her not having close family of her own. The *Comte* being near to death left her with a feeling of mourning felt almost as deeply as *Madame*.

Everyone went about on tiptoe, not that it made a great deal of difference to the house, which was amply furnished with thick carpets and other furnishings calculated to deaden unnecessary noise.

Mike Liddell, who had permitted himself the luxury of a bed in town at the end of his trip to Indian Ridge, presented himself at the house shortly after ten o'clock the next morning. Joseph, the veteran negro butler, welcomed him at the front door and ushered him in.

Mike gripped the old man by the shoulder, asked after the *Comte*'s health, slumped into an upright chair to hear the latest news. Joseph told him of *Madame*'s apparent distraction: how Molly was virtually running things, and expecting him — Mr. Michael — back by the hour.

'Am I right in thinking the under-taker has arrived, Joseph? I thought I heard faint sounds of woodworking comin' from one of the stables.'

'Yes, sir, Mr. Michael, your Mr. Martin, I believe he's called, arrived yesterday with his hearse, his men, wood and tools. I believe they've almost finished preparing a coffin for the head of the house, but they won't be staying.'

'*Madame* is sending them away?' Michael wanted to know.

'It seems so, Mr. Michael. You see, she thinks her father-in-law might last a long time. So, they've dug out the burial plot, prepared the box, and then they'll return to their base. It seems a sensible thing to do.'

Michael thought it over and agreed. He then allowed Joseph to hasten him on his way to the kitchen where, it was thought, Molly had a pressing problem. He pushed open the door, encountered a cloud of steam, and felt a body blunder into him through it.

'Who, who's that, for goodness' sakes? Oh, it's you, Michael. Well, thank goodness for that.'

Molly sounded a little distracted. Carmelita, the maid, flashed Michael a toothy smile through the steamy atmosphere before she was left on her own to cope with washing and meal preparation.

The Irishwoman slid thankfully into his arms, which were held protectively. He had checked his appearance in a mirror before reaching the kitchen and knew that he was looking good with his fair hair well groomed and his chin freshly scraped. Molly glanced up at him, blushed, dodged his all-compelling blue eyes and occupied herself in smoothing down the front of his new blue shirt and adjusting his red bandanna.

'I missed you, Molly,' he murmured, 'Joseph told me most of the details. How are you coping?'

She slipped him a kiss and wriggled free, drawing him across to the sideboard, in the room adjoining the kitchen. Holding a tall glass of amber wine she approached him again. 'Drink this. I wish you could stay around. I could do with a big manly shoulder to rest on now and again.'

He took the glass, sipped at it,

grinned hungrily at her and made her blush again. 'You aren't tryin' to tell me I've got to leave again, are you? I'm gettin' kind of tired about bein' the chateau's out of town representative.'

'I know, I know,' she agreed, shifting her weight from one moccasined foot to the other and nervously adjusting the white lace fastening of her puckered peasant blouse. 'But you'll do this for me, because you're one hell of a man an' I need your help, if I'm not to let *Madame* down.'

Mike took the seat, topped up his own glass of the best sherry, and pulled Molly down on to the seat beside him.

'All right, what's botherin' you?'

'There's a man called Lebrun coming here in the next half hour. *Madame* promised him an escort as far as Pecos Creek or thereabouts. He's to be met by a mounted escort belonging to a security firm. They'll take him across the Pecos river and into the next county further west, where he lives.

'Will you ride with him till he meets

up with his proper escort? *Madame* is afraid he might be waylaid, you see he's carrying valuables, the known proceeds of the late Charles Lebrun's estate.'

Mike's brow clouded, as Molly had known it would. She knew that Mike had been implicated in some way with the 'disappearance' of Sundown's eminent lawyer only a few months earlier. Only Mike, Earl Marden and Marden's men knew where the arch-villain's body lay in a secret place to the north of Sundown.

The late Charles Lebrun had planned the death of the Beauclerc heir, his aim being to marry the widowed *Madame la Baronne*, or get his hands on the family fortune by some foul means or other.

'Is the law office still functioning?' Mike asked thoughtfully.

Molly nodded. 'All *Madame*'s papers have been withdrawn from the firm and are now in the house. The business is being run by young Harry Martlett who was training to be a lawyer under Lebrun. He's managing, all right, backed up by Jones, Lebrun's elderly clerk, and a retired lawyer in town goes in and helps when help is needed.

'This character Andrew Lebrun is the closest known relative. A professional man of some sort, domiciled in the next county. I think he knows there was something unusual about his missing cousin, and he looks to me sometimes as if he is fearful for his life. You *will* see him on his way, won't you, Mike?'

Mike nodded, showing little enthusiasm, and intimated that he would like to speak to his friend, the undertaker, before he had to dash off again out of town. Molly watched him go, and was slightly disappointed.

★　★　★

When Mike Liddell had made contact with Andrew Lebrun, and gone off with him towards the west, time dragged for the regular clientele of the Chateau Beauclerc. Those who loved the old *Comte* felt that they were living on

97

borrowed time. About an hour later, Earl Marden, using his alias of Earl Martin, called upon *Madame* and intimated that he had done all he could in preparing for the old man's demise. *Madeleine de Beauclerc*, although distracted by her emotions, nevertheless thanked him profusely for his attentions, past and present, and sent him back to his base well paid for his efforts.

After that, the only other visitors to the chateau were two young men of the town who had been hastily recruited and drummed into service by Mike Liddell to act as makeshift guards. They appeared around six in the evening and stayed in attendance out at the front, until someone came out and suggested that it was time to secure for the night. This happened usually between ten and eleven o'clock.

On that occasion when Mike had paid his fleeting visit, and the undertaker and his men had quit the property, nothing happened to disturb their spell of duty. It was the following evening, twenty-four hours later, when untoward things started to happen.

About nine in the evening, the three highly-placed lamps which illuminated the main entrances were turned up to give their maximum light. Since the withdrawal of the deceased Lebrun, the wearing of uniform suit for guards had been terminated as a general practice. Consequently, Red Palin, a native of Sundown City, and his cousin, Dixie Mead, who had drifted into town from a state further east, looked more like prosperous cattle operatives than hand-picked gun-toting guards.

Red was taller and thinner than his cousin, but the regulation fawn side-rolled stetsons favoured by both made them look alike, and the padded reinforced jackets usually associated with lumbermen completed the illusion.

They were seated side by side on the front steps when the whistle came from across the tree-lined avenue and alerted them both.

'What do you make of that, Dixie?' Red asked, peering forward to examine the shadowy area beyond the lamplight.

'Maybe something, maybe nothing,' Dixie muttered, snorting through his misshapen nose.

Next came a voice. 'Hey, you guys, could you step over here a minute, give me a hand?'

The voice sounded like a local man, someone with a problem. The cousins eyed each other and slowly stood up. Red, the local man, took the initiative. He glanced north and south along the avenue, then leisurely crossed the thoroughfare with a rifle cradled under his bent right arm.

Still short of the hedge on the other side, he paused, fully on the alert, and cleared his throat. 'Hey, hombre, can you show yourself, an' say what's wrong?'

A few seconds dragged by, during which Dixie walked clear of the corner of the big house and studied the situation from a slightly different angle.

There was a slight movement perhaps ten yards away from Red. His reaction was to shift his feet nervously. He was puzzled.

When Dixie gasped, took a step backwards and went down on his knees, Red was frankly baffled. He turned to face his cousin, wondering what had happened to him. Before he had the chance to enquire, there was a whirring sound, the cause of which was not easily identifiable. Out of the darkness flew a rope and weight contraption which wrapped itself round Red's lower trunk and legs, and threw him to the ground, stunned and winded, and temporarily disarmed.

At the same time, Dixie Mead collapsed in a prone position breathing fitfully and with great difficulty. An agile figure vaulted the hedge from which the attack had come and ran nimbly across the open ground to where Dixie lay.

The silent attacker wore dark clothing. He bent over the stocky body, removed the hat and dragged it by the lumber coat collar into the shelter of the hedge on the nearer side, just north of the building. He was breathing hard when he came back, picked up the fallen rifle and ran back to Red, who was unconscious.

'You might have helped with this one,' he whispered curtly. 'Here, catch this!'

He tossed the rifle over the hedge. Unseen hands caught it, and then a similar weapon which had belonged to Red. The unfortunate Palin was hauled through the prickly hedge and dumped behind it. His attacker worked quickly, trussing and gagging him.

'So what are you waitin' for? Has your blood turned to water again? You see how easy it was. Now, go.'

'I — I can't. There's too much light over there. It only wants for somebody to come to the front of the house, or a casual rider or stroller to come by. You can see how it is, an' *you* of all people wouldn't want me to fail.'

The voice of the second man sounded desperate. In fact, this was the nearest Roxy Barlow had ever been to the Chateau Beauclerc and he had no confidence in what was to follow. His persecutor gathered up the bolas, which had accounted for Red, stared at the offending lamps across the way, and decided to humour his unwilling partner.

Rapidly, he donned the lumber coat which he had taken from Palin and tried on the Texas-style hat. The headgear was really too large for him, but neither of them was in a joking mood. He quickly hauled it into another shape, stuck it on his head, and prepared to move.

'All right. I will see to the lamps. As soon as that is done, you will make your move. Use the method of entry you say your friend did, and remember what you are looking for, in particular. Keep a sharp look out.'

So saying, the leader leapt the hedge, and casually strolled across the avenue, keeping his features in the shadows and trying to look like a regular guard. He found the long pole used to hook down the lamps from their brackets over the entrance, unhooked them, one at a time, turned them low, and hung them back again.

He then cleared his throat in a certain characteristic fashion. Barlow hesitated a few seconds, cleared the hedge with difficulty and ran clumsily across the avenue, going round the end of the building and down the north side of the house. Presently, he located pipe which conducted water from the roof to the ground, and there he paused and looked up.

★   ★   ★

Mike Liddell, returning from his successful mission to the landing stage west of Pecos Creek with the lugubrious Andrew Lebrun, had walked his sweating chestnut horse through the main cluster of town buildings near the western outskirts before turning its head towards the north and the chateau. He was tired, morose and disgruntled. On the journey west, he had travelled the first few miles in the wheeled vehicle favoured by Charles Lebrun's relative, but the fellow had proved so suspicious and so utterly off-putting in his conversation, that Mike had insisted on leaving the vehicle and mounting his horse, which had been trotting behind.

He had passed the one night in Pecos Creek without seeking to rub shoulders with old acquaintances. After breakfasting at a fairly late hour, he had set off back, and here he was with one leg draped round the saddle horn, heading for the chateau only to find out if there was any change in the *Comte*'s condition.

Although he was tired, his senses were on the alert. The chateau had a special atmosphere for him. In this particular evening, when the head of the noble family was near to death, he did not expect an atmosphere like that first occasion when a ball had been in progress.

Nevertheless, he expected to be impressed, somehow. The turned down lamps on the western aspect puzzled him, as he knew exactly what hour it was. Unless the old man had died recently, something was wrong. His instinct told him so. Approaching from the south, he ought to have seen Palin and Mead, and they were nowhere visible.

He slipped his leg back into place, listening and watching for telling signs. Intuition born of experience made him dismount short of the building on the south side and make his way nearer via the wicket gate on that side, and the path to the east.

He ran clear of the north-east corner, paused slightly breathless on a finely trimmed patch of lawn and glanced up towards the top storey. Out of the stillness and pensive quiet of the building's interior, a woman's unrehearsed scream shattered the atmosphere. Mike stiffened. He thought he knew the identity of the screamer.

He had no time to react, however, because a very hard round object hit him violently in the solar plexus and doubled him up in a dead faint on the grass.

7

Patterns of excruciating pain rippled through Mike's body for several minutes before he even started to be aware of his surroundings. He felt as if a cannon ball had passed through him and carried him well on the way to eternity.

Presently, voices he knew began to penetrate his consciousness and he recollected being back at the chateau. By that time, his pains had located themselves in two areas: one in the solar plexus, below his breast-bone, and the other in his head.

He opened his eyes, slowly and with caution, murmuring: 'What happened, Molly?'

At that stage he was not aware of the faintness of his utterance, but the pains down below were aggravated on account of his diaphragm and the talking effort. Old Joseph had brought a basin of warm water with which to bathe his face, forehead and neck.

'You were out in the garden at the time, Mike. Something hit you. A ball of metal. We believe you blundered on an intruder!'

The sort of nausea which Mike associated with vomiting began to assail him. His small movements told him he had been placed in a *chaise-longue* located in a glassed-in verandah on the side of the house.

'Molly, I feel terrible. But what of *Madame*, of the house? Did the intruder get in?'

The young Irishwoman, fearing that he would faint again, had backed away to get some smelling salts. It was Joseph who answered.

'Yes, Mr. Michael, a man entered by the window of *Madame*'s bedroom. He is up there now, but he appears to have suffered a mortal wound. I think there was another person around. But who struck down the one upstairs is a mystery.'

From the interior of the house came an anguished cry. *Madame*'s cultured voice was greatly distorted by the strain she was under.

'This man will not live much longer! Somebody do something!'

The servants were filled with mounting consternation, particularly because *Madame* had imposed a ban on all shouting and noisy music since the beginning of *Monsieur le Comte*'s seizure. Racing footsteps came down the thickly carpeted stairs, and the well-rounded teenage figure of Carmelita, the maid, bounced against the slimmer one of Molly O'Callan, who was returning with smelling salts.

The young Mexican girl gave ground to Molly, who frowned at her. Together, they approached the *chaise-longue*, where Joseph — jacketless and perspiring — mopped his heated brow. The jet-black centrally parted hair of the Mexican girl mingled with the long copper-coloured tresses which were

Molly's crowning glory.

Mike stayed the hand that held the smelling salts long enough to give Carmelita an enquiring glance.

'It is the intruder, *Senor* Mike, the burglar. He is very low, but he asks for *you*. I heard him with my own ears, close to the carpet. *Madame* will not believe me, but it true. She also needs help. She is faint . . . '

Mike, Molly and Joseph were all remarkably startled when they heard the panting girl's revelations. Mike grabbed the smelling salts, sniffed them until his pale blue eyes watered. He signified his intention of getting up to the next floor to speak with the intruder before the latter expired. One after the other, the trio backed off, each aware of his sorry condition. When he writhed and almost fell off the *chaise-longue* Molly signalled for Joseph and the girl to support him. She herself, headed them up the staircase to where *Madame* was alone in her bedroom with the wounded man.

Mike's stomach lurched several times before they reached the upper level. It was all he could do to keep the contents of an earlier meal in place, but eventually they reached *Madame*'s bedroom and his two supporters lowered him on to the light-coloured carpet where the man in soiled trail garb lay with blood steadily seeping through his multi-coloured shirt and on to the carpet.

Madame had withdrawn to a wicker chair placed near the open window. She had suffered several shocks of late. First, her father-in-law's seizure, then this burglarious entry, and now a suggestion that the man dying on her bedroom carpet was known to *Michel* (Michael) who was high in her trust and close in her affections.

Mike's condition drew an anguished look from the lady of the house, but at the same time the dying intruder repelled her. In spite of the Beauclerc menfolks' long term association with battles and gore, she was not at her best in the presence of blood.

Poised on hands and knees beside the fallen man, Mike Liddell absorbed his biggest shock of the evening. He was looking into the stricken face of Roxy Barlow, the man he had left behind in Eastville with a woman on his mind. The one thing he had asked of Roxy was to stay away from the Chateau Beauclerc, and here he was, dying on *Madame*'s bedroom carpet.

Mike had to throw up. He moved away on hands and knees and did what he had to do into a bucket provided by the butler. Nothing would have made him perform such an act in the presence of these three women. Only the imminent death of Roxy Barlow kept him from staggering to the nearest bathroom.

Molly bathed his face with a cloth and then backed away to use the smelling salts on her mistress.

Mike said: 'Roxy, until now, I have never really rued the day I met you, but I do now. If you have the strength, tell me why and how this has happened.

You owe me that much, I think.'

Another spasm gripped the young Texan, effectively stopping his emotive words. Mike took a cloth from Carmelita and used it to wipe Roxy's lips. They gave him a small drink of water, and all assembled awaited developments. Mike had to put his face close, as Carmelita had done earlier.

'I, I was forced to do it, Mike. And I'm sorry. Trouble . . . in Eastville.'

A tiny trickle of blood came freshly from the corner of the mouth. It coursed down a wrinkle in the weathered skin and gathered around the stubbled chin.

'Who forced you, and why, Roxy,' Mike raised his voice. 'Make the effort, for goodness' sake. Who?'

'A . . . a Frenchman, Name of . . . Ramon. Used to be in the Foreign Legion.'

Roxy's eyes closed with the effort he had made. Mike studied him, ignoring his own nausea. As near as he could judge, Roxy had been wounded in the shoulder by a knife. The wound had gone deep and, presumably, severed an artery. It occurred to Mike that someone in the room had possibly removed the weapon from the wound, and then his thoughts blurred. He didn't know why the knifer shouldn't have hauled it clear himself.

Roxy Barlow came back from the brink of death. Mike tried again, hating himself as he continued his questioning, hating everything that had happened to him of late.

'Why did he send you in here? What did he want.'

Even as he asked the last question, fleeting thoughts of all the possible treasures in that house of houses skimmed through his brain.

Roxy organised his remaining strength. '*He was a paint . . . wanted a paint . . .* '

He seemed fated not to finish his revelation and, knowing the end was upon him he feebly raised an arm and gestured in a wavering arc which seemed to take in the wall space behind the ornate metal bed and the nearby open window. Mike was baffled, the more so when Roxy's limp arm flopped down again and his old friend and comrade of the trails expired with a long shuddering gasp.

In an effort to do something positive, Mike raised himself to his feet unaided. As a direct result, fresh spasms of pain radiated from his mid-riff and his senses floated away, as on a cloud.

For a short time, the three women and the old negro butler were bereft of speech and totally incapable of action.

8

Mike Liddell did not remember anyone having given him anything to dope him, but he soon discovered how much time had passed when Molly unceremoniously swished aside the curtains of the downstairs guest bedroom and allowed the sunshine to illuminate the interior of the tastefully furnished chamber.

Mike blinked, felt the bandaging around his waist, winced and coughed. 'Molly, is that you?'

'I don't know many other folks it could be, trouble-shooter,' she retorted curtly. 'I suppose I ought to ask you how are you feelin'?'

'Doped, pained and weak, me darlin',' he remarked, feeling himself over, carefully. 'How much time have I been out of action?'

'The so-called burglary happened the night before last. This is eight o'clock in the morning. Can you eat, do you think?'

'I suppose so, but if I knew the answers to a few questions I reckon my appetite would improve.'

Molly had her hair pulled back in a pony's tail held by a green ribbon. She glanced at him from time to time, but all the while she was flicking away at dusty surfaces with a square of cloth.

'What about the man who was knifed? Has he — '

'He's not been buried, if that's what's botherin' you. *Madame* has had him boxed by the local man, although I can tell you she didn't relish it. Him, and the new town marshal, all bluster an' moustache, an' that other bearded weasel, Shamus Flint, from the *Sundown Bugle*.

'As you probably know, she hates the locals gettin' their noses into Beauclerc private business, but on this occasion she had no alternative, you bein' her protector of sorts an' bein' in the condition you were.'

Mike hauled himself up on an elbow. 'Now hold on Molly, you surely didn't think I took that blow in the stomach on purpose? The happenings of the other night baffled me as much as they did anybody else.'

'But you did know the man who broke in,' Molly retorted bitingly. 'It was you he asked for when he was dyin', an' that has to mean something,' she added, hands on shapely hips.

'Molly, I swear to you, I've done nothin', nothin' at all to bring trouble on this house since I first undertook to look for Dickie Beauclerc! And that's the whole truth, so help me.'

The angry Irishwoman tapped the floor with a moccassined toe and frowned at him. 'Knowin' your family like I did, I guess you're speakin' the truth. All the same, the Irish are a superstitious race, an' I'd say you brought bad luck on the Beauclercs the minute you arrived.'

'Superstitious they may be, but your suggestion is unkind. The Beauclercs had troubles before I ever arrived on the scene!' Mike gasped. 'I'm not in a fit state to argue with you. If you'll make me a spot of breakfast, I'll be out of the house an' arrange for the burial as soon as possible. And I'll foot the bill, too.'

'I'll make your breakfast, but get it through your head that things have changed. Right now, all *Madame* can think is that you're a close buddy of an undesirable, who died violently on the premises after breaking in. You're not to go near her. She's very much under the weather, and her confidence in you has been completely shattered.'

Some fifteen minutes later, Mike breakfasted rather uncomfortably under the reproachful gaze of Molly and Carmelita. The Mexican girl looked as if she wanted to be friendly, but Molly's hard expression prevented any softening on the part of the maid.

Mike took his chances to settle a few more items.

'Molly, I want you to make it clear to

Madame — when the time is ripe — that I shall be shoulderin' the responsibility for Barlow's breakin' in, an' I shan't rest until I know who made him do it. You *would* tell me if you knew of anything at all that was missin'. Wouldn't you?'

Molly nodded. 'All right, I'll tell you that much. But the best thing for you to do, if you want my advice, is to resume movin' from place to place like you used to do. I can't make my own attitude clearer than that, can I, now?'

Mike said: 'Molly, you always look your best when you're angry. But this is no time to be flippant. Say, have you thought there may yet be some unknown threat to the Beauclerc family? And what's more I might be the only one in a position to find out what it is, from what direction trouble may come!'

Molly was convinced. Fear changed the steadfast look in her clear green eyes. 'I — I'd like to go on believin' in you, Michael Liddell, but you put a strain on the sort of relationships *I* favour. We'll just have to see the way things turn out. Nothin' can improve *Madame*'s condition while the *Comte* lingers on. Any other setback to her could do very serious harm . . . '

At that point, the laundry started to bubble over, and the fleeting conversation had to be curtailed.

★ ★ ★

Moving slowly, and with due consideration for his still painful solar plexus, Mike made it out of the house fully dressed. He saddled up the chestnut, which seemed to be more mobile under him than usual, due to his pains, and rode off to the town centre.

There, he contacted the local undertaker, the town marshal, the newspaper editor, and the two men he had employed as guards for the chateau. The stocky guard, Dixie Mead, was still out of action. The flying metal ball, fashioned with a hole through the middle, had not only put him down and out: it had fractured two of his ribs, as well. Dixie, therefore, was still trussed up, and unable to take any active part in the follow-up to the disturbing events.

Red Palin, however, had recovered. Over coffee, he was able to tell Mike a thing or two about the attack on them before he got back from his escort work. Moreover, Red had in his possession the actual bolas which had suddenly trussed him and knocked him to the ground, unconscious.

Mike intimated that he, too, had been put out of action by a metal ball, and he wondered aloud who in the district was likely to use a cowboy weapon usually associated with the gauchos of South America.

'If you ask me, Mike, I'd say there's a stranger in the district. Unless you think the dead man could have done it.'

The young Texan pushed back his hat and massaged his forehead.

'No, the dead man couldn't have

done it, Red. As a matter of fact, I knew him well. We were ridin' together when the two of us first hit this town. Roxy Barlow had no skill with a bolas, or the weights fashioned to be used with it. As you say, there's a stranger around, somewhere.

'Somebody who's got designs on Beauclerc property. What and why, I don't know. This far, nothin' seems to be missin'. But I guess we'll find out, sooner or later. So you'll be in a position to side me at the burial, mid-afternoon?'

Palin, who had doubts which he would not voice about some of Mike's old comrades, nevertheless, confirmed that he would attend the burial service alongside of the man who had been instrumental in getting him the chateau job in the first place.

A search of the town failed to turn up the regular local parson. Mike began to wonder if he was deliberately keeping out of the way. Had he been warned off, or did he have a conscience problem about saying Christian prayers over criminals?

The knowledge that he would have to say the prayers himself stiffened Mike's resistance to the rigours of the day. He returned briefly to the chateau, determined to go through with the burial, even though help was grudgingly given. After hitching his horse, he went to the rear door, where Joseph admitted him. Clearly, the old negro was in something of a quandary. He was hoping that he would not have to refuse any request by this young man who had so recently lost face.

Mike licked his lips. 'Joseph, I'll be runnin' the burial this afternoon. Before that, I need a bit of help. I want a prayer book, a bath and a brief word with *Monsieur le Comte*. Ask Molly if it is in order. I won't go up to his room if they don't approve.'

Joseph was smiling gently about the first two requests. It was not until the *Comte* was mentioned that he looked worried. He retreated to the kitchen and was slow to return. Acting upon impulse, he followed the old man's footsteps and was in time to witness the copper-haired Irish woman with her teeth clenched and her shapely frame rigid in denial.

'Joseph, you know as well as I do *Madame* said Michael was to be banned from the upper floors. That isn't much of a punishment for a man who admitted to being a close friend of the burglar, now, is it?'

Mike coughed. 'I'm sorry to barge in, Molly. Deny me the bath an' the prayer book, if you must, but I really do need to make contact with the *Comte*. I know certain things about the man who planned the raid on the house. The *Comte*'s mind is better on old items than on recent ones. All I want to do is ask him about a possible family enemy. Can you deny me the right to see him?'

'It isn't easy to communicate with the old man any more. Besides *Madame* has denied you access. He used to look forward to your company, though. I don't want to know if you go upstairs. We'll run you a bath in the downstairs wash house. Don't go. I have something for you.'

She turned to a drawer in a huge article of furniture. From the section next to the carving knives she produced something wrapped in a cotton square. Mike took it, and unwrapped it. He did not need to be told about it. He was looking at a finely balanced thin-bladed dagger with what looked like bony grips on the handle. A useful weapon for close-fighting of a certain type. It also might have another use.

'Where was it, Molly?' he asked, frowning.

'In your friend's neck, Mike, or very close.' Molly sighed. She had wanted to punish him by bringing up the association with Barlow again, but her gaze softened and her fiery eyes moistened. For a few seconds, she could not quite weigh up his reaction. He seemed pleased, almost, although only one who knew him well would have known by his changing expression.

Seated on the edge of an upright chair, Mike fumbled with his boots, having discarded his spurs. Molly was warring with herself. She would have liked to assist him in his struggle with the unyielding leather.

'What is it?' she asked.

'This is the type of knife that could have been thrown by someone out in the garden. Probably the same man who is skilful with a bolas, and in hurling metal balls. I'll be down for the bath in just a few minutes.'

With a curt nod, he tiptoed out of the room and ran up the stairs without a sound. He knew the room where the old man was, and he entered without knocking. *Monsieur le Comte de Beauclerc* was propped up with an extra pillow. His metal rimmed spectacles were propped on his eagle's beak of a nose, but he was not reading. Paralysis had deprived him of natural movement below the waist. He could not speak, and only one hand functioned feebly with a great effort.

Mike stood beside the bed and was rewarded by a warm regard from the eyes magnified by the lenses. He knelt, noticed that the old man's means of communication was rather primitive. All he had to do was press the top of his head against the headboard and that would start a small hand bell ringing. Mike hoped he would not ring it accidentally for a few minutes.

'*Monsieur le Comte*, you can hear me?' he whispered.

The old man blinked positively. Mike grasped the wrinkled right hand, felt a response. He murmured briefly how sorry he was that the *Comte* was so badly stricken, went on to explain that there had been a burglary and that he — *Michael* — had lost face because he knew the intruder of old.

He went on: 'Nothing was stolen that we know of, and the intruder was killed by a knife, handled by an unknown assailant.'

He paused, unwrapped the blade and

put it in a position where the *Comte* could see it. There was an instant reaction.

'The dying man mentioned someone called Ramon, who had forced him to enter the building. This is why I am here. I think this Ramon may wish the family harm. I believe he was in the *Légion Étrangère*, and there is some connection with South America. Do you know of any such person?'

The *Comte* blinked several times. Mike was pleased, but it took a few seconds for him to get round to what the old man wanted. Presently the visitor had a big scribbling pad of paper on a board sufficiently close to the right side of the bed for the old man to write on it with a pencil.

The effort which was needed to write brief phrases embarrassed the younger man, but gradually the information was written.

'*Ramon Perrier, a great nephew. Painter. Bad Lot. Some scandal in Paris. Joined the Legion. Started well, then quit. Escaped. To South America. To be avoided.'*

Mike read over the words written down, so that the wearying old man could confirm them. As a final gesture, the *Comte* put his pencil through the word 'painter' and Mike then gave up his quest for information, fearing that he might overtax the old fellow and bring about his instant demise.

After assuring the *Comte* of his continued devotion, Mike shook his hand again, showed him the Beauclerc ring on his finger and quietly withdrew from the room, closing the door behind him. He slipped the ring off his finger, as he considered it was better not to wear it in the bath.

* * *

The burial was really a non-event. The cortege, if it could be so named, started outside the Second Street building belonging to the undertaker. The hearse was an old farmer's cart cleaned up for the occasion, manned by the under-taker and two casual assistants.

Town Marshal Abel Smith, of the stiff leg and even stiffer greying handlebar moustache, shared a perch on the broad seat of a buckboard with his friend and drinking crony, bearded Shamus Flint of the *Sundown Bugle*. Red Palin and Mike were the only two mounted riders, except for two Mexican chateau gardeners who brought up the rear on mules.

Perhaps two dozen townsfolk on foot watched the cortege take off, but none of them followed it the half mile out of town towards Boot Hill, which was situated north of west. The burial ground was nicely kept. Like most western towns, it had a select section for those who only just merited interment in hallowed ground.

Mike's oration was rather more of a testimony to the deceased's good character before the time when another took over his will and ruined him than a funeral speech. Being slightly carried away with his own words, and mindful of the town marshal getting an earful, Mike added that it was his intention to keep asking questions and looking about the county until such time as he located the villain who had murdered Roxy Barlow on Beauclerc territory.

The prayers, when the time came, rolled off his tongue as they had from the lips of his father, who, as well as being a medical man, had been very religious.

The proceedings were soon over, and Mike left the filling in of the grave to the gardeners. For a minute or two, the assembled mourners gathered together.

Town Marshal Smith leaned his back against the dry-stone wall and twirled his moustache. 'I'd like to make it clear, young fellow, that when a criminal is killed in the act of committing a crime, an official in my office is not required to search out the killer.

'All the same, I've made known the facts as I was told them to the county sheriff's office.'

Mike, who still had twinges from his injured mid-riff, fought down an inclination to bandy words with the local man. 'I'm sure you've taken all steps your office requires you to, marshal. Now, if you'll excuse me, I'll high-tail it down the hill an' start lookin' around for strangers.'

Smith dug Flint in the ribs, as he swung his game leg up on to the buckboard. 'I hope the countess is payin' you well to keep lookin'!' he called to Mike.

Mike and Palin had forked their horses together. They exchanged glances. Shamus Flint looked as if he would have liked an argument to develop. Perhaps such a move would have given him some gossip for his paper.

Mike replied: 'If it's of any interest to you, marshal, I shall not be takin' any payment for this job. The man we've just buried was my friend. A word of advice, steer clear of a man who throws lethal objects. Knives, metal balls an' such like. I don't think you'd stand a chance of gettin' clear, if he took a fancy to you.'

While Smith was catching his breath, Mike touched his hat and walked his horse off down the slope, following Palin.

In a minute or two, he regretted having taunted the lawman over his lack of mobility. Even though the fellow had deliberately set out to rile him. Back in town, Red and Mike parted. The latter spent two hours scouring every public building and boarding house.

There was no one in the township who could possibly fill the vague description of the man he sought.

9

That same night, Mike rode again to the site of Boot Hill and used the high ground to survey the territory round about in case Barlow's missing associate had simply pulled out of town and made camp. He saw no signs of night fires and, consequently, he retired early, using a warm spot in the local smithy as a temporary shakedown.

Jock McArthur, the bulky smith, always drank a lot of beer in the early evening to counteract his perspiring in the day. Jock, then, had turned in long before Mike arrived to occupy a warm part of his domain. The beer also made the smith a slow starter in the morning.

Towards eight a.m., Mike was sitting up in his straw bunk, drawing gently on a small cigar and going over the traumatic experiences and revelations of the last few days, when a light footstep approached the outer door and opened it.

The seasoned, seamed face under the steeple hat was that of the older of the gardeners who had helped out at Boot Hill. The appearance of the old man, whose communications were limited almost entirely to Spanish, surprised Mike, who was not sure about his present standing at the chateau.

The old man came inside, nodding and smiling and offering a folded note on Beauclerc headed notepaper. It was from Molly.

Dear Mike,

While you were hunting for a man who throws things an elderly Frenchman who claims to be Henri, Marquis de Louvain, came into town from the west. He is crossing the States from west to east and actually heading for New Orleans. Is going to write a travel book when he gets back to Paris. In order to get rid of him without delay, Madame had to promise a travelling companion who can speak French. She wants you to ride in the coach with him as far as Big Springs, Texas. By the time you get back, the affairs of the Beauclercs may have undergone more changes.

His coach will arrive at nine o'clock.

Love. Molly. X

Mike stretched, yawned and nodded to the mature delivery boy, who beamed back at him and lifted his big hat.

'*Si, si, amigo, comprendo. Adios.*'

He gave the fellow a half dollar and waved him away. McArthur asked who was calling without opening his eyes, and Mike told him to sleep on: that it was not important. He left a coin to cover his night's lodging, checked that his horse was all right on the tiny patch of grass behind the smithy, and went off in search of food.

★   ★   ★

The Marquis of Louvain was a tall, thin, stooping character of around fifty years. The fair hair was sparse on his egghead skull. His grey eyes were deeply eroded. He had a twitching upper lip. His nose was the Syrian type with a drooping septum. He tended to regard the world with patrician disgust.

All this Mike noted as the fellow stepped into view from the front of the chateau. The dark suit, silk hat and frockcoat looked expensive, but appeared to have suffered during their owner's travels. So had the two carpet bags and the cabin trunk already loaded on the overland coach by the poker-faced guard and driver.

He had a fussy, high-pitched voice. '*Merci mille fois, Madame. Au 'voir a tous.*' He raised his hat, touched *la Baronne*'s limp hand to his lips. Mike, who had attached his saddleless horse to the boot, merited only a passing glance standing there in his trail garb.

Feeling slightly affronted, Mike allow-ed the fellow to stumble up the folding steps of the coach and get in unaided.

Mike thought *la Baronne's* beauty and elegance was in no way impaired by recent events, although she did have marked grey shadows under her remarkable blue eyes. She was wearing a short-sleeved blue velvet house-coat and matching mules, with her hair piled high and pinned.

'*Madame*, I am sorry for what happened in and around your house of late. This, this escort duty would not have been of my choice of work, at the moment. I think I could possibly have been of more service nearer at hand.'

Mike moved closer, as though he would have kissed her hand, but she withdrew slightly, indicating that she did not wish it.

'I may be wrong about you, and about recent events, *Michel*. There are so many happenings in my life at the moment, I am no longer able to think clearly. In escorting this French gentleman, you will still be serving the house.'

Mike smiled gravely. 'I know, but that

was not what I had in mind when I promised *Monsieur le Comte* yesterday that I would continue to protect you.'

Madeleine de Beauclerc showed mild surprise at this revelation. She licked her lips and appeared for a moment as if she would unbend and show Mike a little of her old warmth, but the effort on this occasion was too much for her. The Marquis of Louvain was calling out in a querulous voice, wanting to know where his French-speaking travelling companion had got to. The pair in front of the house completely ignored him.

Almost as an afterthought, *Madame* gestured round the side of the house. 'Go round to the other door, *Michel*. Molly has one or two things for you. You mustn't miss saying goodbye to her, in any case.'

Giving him a last grudging smile, the lady of the house stepped indoors. Mike hesitated for a few seconds and then went round to the entrance nearest to the kitchen. Molly opened the door as he arrived and almost fell into his arms with a basket of fresh food, prepared especially for the journey.

Her true feelings showed. 'Mike, I thought you'd gone without . . . your personal belongings. We have your things rolled for the saddle, although I'm not much good at saddle rolls. And those items of food should help pass the time with a boring old man.'

Carmelita moved past them with the saddle roll clutched diagonally across her bosom. She murmured: '*Hasta la vista, Senor* Mike,' in lisping Spanish, and left them alone.

Mike said: 'If there is any sort of threat while I am away, you must break *Madame's* rules and bring in the local peace officers. The security is no longer sound.'

'I know you are right, but you frighten me so, talkin' that way. Here, take the basket. There is a packet of dollars in there. Take them and use them. No man works for nothing, even if he is angry with his employer. And take care of yourself. *Au revoir.*'

What Molly had intended for a brief kiss lengthened into a short passionate hug more like a lover's embrace. But they parted quickly, the woman to go indoors and the man to return hurriedly to the front of the house with the food basket.

Mike leapt up the steps of the conveyance in one bound, and signified that he was ready to go. His roll had already been slung on the top and secured. Carmelita hovered about, waving and walking backwards. *Madame* reappeared at the front door, and Molly suddenly showed herself at a first floor window.

Mike sighed with a certain amount of relief. For a fellow who was under a cloud of sorts, they were showing a lot of interest. As the coach lurched off, he formally introduced himself to the fussy passenger, shook the tentatively offered hand, and sat down.

The Marquis watched him as he produced the envelope from the basket, opened it and stared at the wad of dollar bills. Presently, Mike stuffed them into the pocket of his shirt and lost interest in them.

The Marquis remarked in piping French: 'So, a paid servant of the family.'

Mike, thoroughly annoyed, answered him in French. 'I could leave at any time I want, *Monsieur le Marquis*, but I choose to stay. And I accept money for odious tasks.'

This cutting rejoinder had the immediate effect of starting the Frenchman coughing. It also suspended conversation for quite a time. An hour later, the grumbling started. Most of it was centred around the state of the track and the quality of the driving. After a time, Mike relayed the complaints up to the box, and when that did not improve matters the Marquis tentatively suggested that Mike might like to take over the reins.

The Texan accepted the challenge. He knew that the driver and the guard were of the opinion that he was no better than any other dude in western garb. Mike had a chip on his shoulder about the dude tag, and explained what the V.I.P. passenger wanted. They stopped, the driver handed over the reins with his big greying moustache scarcely masking his grin of triumph, and the journey was resumed.

The guard was the first to realise that Mike knew exactly what he was doing. After a time, the young Texan rocked the coach deliberately and generally made the going difficult for those travelling inside.

The passenger grumbled a few times, apparently unheard and it was the driver who eventually made a change through his loudly-worded protests. As they came to a halt beside water, the driver protested that there was no peace in the interior with the old French fool, and Mike had to agree.

A walk in the fresh air and a picnic lunch helped to put everybody in a better humour.

During the afternoon, a form of exhaustion prevented the travellers from quarrelling. Mike dozed fitfully and ignored his companion's efforts at barbed conversation. Little Springs, the half way stage of the journey, rolled into view around six in the evening, and that was the signal for everyone to show a little more interest in life.

They parted outside a reasonably appointed hotel where the two main thoroughfares, north-south and east-west crossed each other. Mike was the first to go. He walked the chestnut horse away to a stable at the eastern end, while the coach team unloaded Louvain's luggage into the nearest building.

Mike found for himself a smaller hotel located in the eastern half of Main. There, he took a bath, changed and consumed his evening meal. The Marquis was rather surprised to see him appear in the lounge of the larger hotel two hours later. Having failed to make the acquaintance of the two most affluent travelling groups, Louvain was inclined to be pleasant.

Mike suggested a game of chess. It was a good idea. Louvain fancied himself as a player. It was one of the few activities which occupied all his faculties and stopped him making critical remarks about everything and everybody.

In just over an hour, Mike cornered the Frenchman's king, and that result had the effect of putting him much higher in his opponent's estimation. The second game started just as tensely, but after a while the rigours of the day began to affect Louvain's concentration.

He dozed briefly on two occasions. Mike did not bother to rouse him. After the second unplanned interlude the Marquis turned obdurate.

'I hate to have to say this, Liddell, but you must have shifted the pieces when I was dozing.'

Mike stared at him, hard. He then lifted the board, half folded it together and tipped the pieces into his opponent's lap.

'Louvain, you are a bad loser, as well as being a frightful bore and a bad mixer. I can't think why anyone would want to read a travel book penned by yourself. Goodnight.'

Mike left the building, sought out the coach crew and bought them a couple of drinks each, which had the effect of making them think he was much more human than they had first estimated.

★　★　★

The second leg of the gruelling journey, from Little Springs, New Mexico territory, all the way to the Texas border, and a short journey beyond, was a much worse endurance test than the first leg had been. The crew suffered through the jerking, bumping, dust and a lack of fresh water at a time when it was most needed.

Molly O'Callan's fresh food supply had long since been consumed and that worsened the conditions for the travellers. The Marquis was rather less a nuisance than before, simply because no one would be a scapegoat and stay near him long enough for him to swamp them in complaints.

Mike ignored his protests when he made it clear that he was going to ride his horse for most of the way. Up on the chestnut's back, he had freedom of a sort. He could ride ahead, or drop way back behind. Mostly, he chose to be in front, because that way he could avoid the dust put up by the milling hooves and the coach's wheels.

Louvain made one valiant attempt to get attention and help around seven o'clock in the evening, over the Texas border. He leaned out of the coach, waved his fist and yelled at Mike, as the latter rode past.

'I demand to be let out of this bucking tumbrel for a change of scene and a rest!'

'There is no such thing as a change of scene in this part of the Lone Star state, amigo. Moreover, if you don't stop grumbling I will instruct the crew to dump you here and let you walk!'

The guard dug the driver in the ribs, and he winked cautiously at the young Texan as he cantered ahead.

On arrival in Big Springs, Mike stayed near the Frenchman until he had seen the crew paid their just wages. He then curtly took his leave of the traveller and went on a walking tour of the saloons. He soon found confirmation of something he had known for a long time. The beer in Texas did not taste any better than that in New Mexico.

Reduced to his own company, Mike started back around eight in the morning, determined to make ground back to the chateau with all haste. It was easier, on his own, to brood over the happenings which had led to Roxy Barlow's startling reappearance, and that same character's demise.

As the miles of dust rolled by under him, he had a deep sense of foreboding:

a feeling that something untoward was about to happen at the Beauclerc house while he was still more than a day's ride away.

His shirt was soaked around the shoulders several times, only to be dried out again by the heat of the sun. By the time Little Springs hove into sight about seven in the evening, he had decided to investigate the town of Eastville, where Roxy had claimed his troubles started.

Horse and man were drooping as they plodded up Main Street, anything but fresh from the energy-sapping trail. This time, Mike walked his light brown horse all the way to the other end, from which he could quit the town easily, if and when he managed to drum up sufficient energy to resume. He surrendered his horse, informed the ostler that he might start out again, later that same evening, and then withdrew to seek some comfort for himself.

He had just paused to shift the saddle from one shoulder to the other when his idle glance took in one or two collector's pieces in a neatly dressed shop window. The portrait of an elegant woman, seated in all her finery for a special occasion, was just one more item to rest the eyes on. Until he looked closer, drawn against his tired inclination to be on his way.

It was an exceedingly good likeness. *Madeleine, la Baronne de Beauclerc*, always looked good in oils. In fact, she always looked good in the eyes of the beholder, whatever she was doing or preparing for.

Mike dropped the saddle heavily to the boards and looked closer. She was wearing a sort of cream-coloured satin dress, skimpy over the shoulders and daringly revealing over the cleavage. The lower part of her becoming expression showed a half smile, while the unique blue eyes held the eye of the painter, and of the beholder.

Fine white elbow length gloves and the cut glass earrings she favoured added to the general effect, and a wide blue sash, loosely draped across the bosom from the left shoulder finished off the total effect.

Mike tried the shop door and found it locked. He sighed, and picked up his saddle.

10

More than twelve hours later, Mike made it into the shop, at once explained what he wanted and had the picture removed from the shop window. The proprietor was an unusual character for that part of the world. A cultured old German, who padded about in mocassins, his bulky stooping body wrapped around with a padded silk smoking jacket, and his bald head pushed into a skull cap decorated with eastern designs.

'Thirty dollars, sir, to a purchaser of discernment,' the old man suggested.

'Twenty dollars would be nearer the true value,' Mike argued, with folding money held in one hand.

The old man wagged an admonishing finger at him. 'Come now, the frame itself is worth ten dollars.'

Mike flashed his most captivating

smile, which had an effect of sorts. 'I don't want the frame, only the canvas. But I will give you twenty-five dollars if you tell me something about the picture itself.'

The shopkeeper looked doubtful for a while, but he agreed. His face was very expressive when the questioning began, and a certain deafness appeared to grow conveniently worse when he did not want to answer. Not much headway about how the painting came into the shopkeeper's possession, but a very definite assurance that it had not been painted recently. It was anything from two to five years old.

Mike sighed, frowned, handed over the agreed figure and left in a hurry. The picture had been stripped off the cheap frame and rolled up in a protective tube for easy carrying. When he left the town, Mike had it strapped to his back. The distance by trail back to Sundown was every bit as far, but the time seemed not to drag so much. The discovery of the painting had made

Mike feel that his protracted ride away from the chateau had not been wasted. He kept remembering Roxy's last words. Something about a painting, or was it a painter?

Not knowing quite what his old partner had in mind annoyed him, but coupled with the coincidental discovery of *Madame's* painting in a nearby town, he felt that he would soon make progress, that he stood a chance of clearing up the mystery surrounding Roxy's death.

Eventually, he made it into Sundown by a little after six in the evening. Pausing only to sluice himself down under a pump, he walked his horse in the direction of the chateau without benefit of beer. Around the front, he was in for a surprise.

Red Palin, one of the guards he had appointed himself, was nowhere in evidence. Nor was Red's cousin, who had suffered a bad rib injury. But there were two strangers in the position of guards fronting the house and giving anyone who went near more than a casual scrutiny.

He listened to what they said to each other as he approached. They whispered to one another in French. Not the Parisian French of the boulevards, more like a French-Canadian *patois*, or even the special way of talking adopted by non-Frenchmen to get themselves by in the Foreign Legion.

Anticipating trouble, he addressed them quietly in French.

'*Bon soir, mes amis*, I am Michael Liddell, friend and confidant of *Madame la Baronne*. Please announce me.'

He swung confidently to the ground and found a bayonet not far from his unprotected back. He protested with a hand gesture.

'*Montez, montez, mon Liddell*,' the shorter of the two ordered, 'we have heard of you. No visitors tonight. *Madame* is resting. *Monsieur* Ramon is painting in the rear garden. No one to be disturbed.'

The mention of the name, *Ramon*,

sent a peculiar sensation up and down the Texan's spine. So, his forebodings had not been without grounds. The mysterious Ramon was already on the premises. And, to cap everything, he was a painter. A good deal had happened in the relatively short time he had been away.

Mike mounted up again, his thoughts seething. 'And if I have valuable properties for *Madame*?'

The taller one, with the blue-black jowl, answered this time: 'So, it is no problem. Hand over the properties to us. We will deliver them.'

Mike backed the tired chestnut a yard or so, at the same time shaking his head. 'Would I surrender *Madame's* valuables to the *Bat d'Af*? No chance, my friend. Maybe tomorrow one of the townsmen will deliver, eh? *Adieu.*'

One of the guards got so far as to click back the hammer of a revolver, but it was not fired. The reference to the *Bat d'Af* had been a casual insult. The *Bataillon d'Afrique* was a criminal military unit made up of law-breakers. Mike rode back into the town centre with a lot on his mind.

This refusal of entry was like history repeating itself, because he had received similar treatment when he first sought to gain entry to the chateau. In fact, that initial rebuff had been the reason for his gate-crashing the Beauclerc ball at the outset. What a long time it seemed since that moment of destiny.

* * *

Mike left his mount and saddle on Jock McArthur's smithy patch. He then wandered back up the street and headed for the bar where he had first started to learn things about the famed Chateau Beauclerc. Jock, himself, was in the Sundowner, property of a veteran Australian named Bluey Darwin. After greeting the Scottish blacksmith and buying him a refill of beer, Mike parked himself on one of the bar stools and engaged the attention of the homely looking character from down-under.

'What do you want to know, sport?'

Bluey massaged the bar with a soiled cloth.

'Two ex-soldiers in long greatcoats and small forage caps, guardin' the big house like Lebrun's boys used to do. What can you tell me about them, Bluey?'

The first time the Australian had fed information to Mike he had done it in a taunting fashion, positive that no one in earshot would succeed in getting into the chateau. Mike, of course, had proved him wrong, and since then Bluey owed him grudging respect.

'Ex-soldiers, yes. French Foreign Legion, I'd say. Don't know where their boss raked em' up from, though.'

'*Monsieur Ramon?*' Mike prompted.

Old Jock eyed him as though he was talking about phantoms, but Bluey had had his ear to the ground. 'Yer, *Monsieur Ramon*. A painter, by all accounts. On the make, I'd say. Gone down big with the *Madame*, I believe, who was feelin' so low because of her father-in-law's imminent death. From what I've heard this Ramon is givin' the orders now. Have you had any trouble with him?'

Upwards of a dozen drinkers stilled their tongues to hear Mike's reply. He was aware of their interest.

'His soldier boys have refused me admittance, but that's happened before. I'll be in there tomorrow, one way or another, don't you grieve!'

This positive suggestion let loose a whole lot of drinkers' banter. Jock wanted to make bets that his friend would achieve an entry, whatever the odds. Mike dissuaded him with difficulty, bought him more beer and slipped away from the bar at the first opportunity.

★ ★ ★

Mike chose his time well, the next morning. At nine a.m., he felt sure that *Madame* and her new friend would be

161

breakfasting in a room at the back of the building. It was then that he had Red Palin drive the light tradesman's cart up to the front of the house and stop there.

Although he was wearing dark headgear and a different coloured shirt, Mike, who shared the box, kept his face averted as the guards appeared. Red showed the shorter man an envelope and the Beauclerc ring off Mike's finger. Acting as though he expected to be allowed to visit the kitchen, Red succeeded in having the short guard deliver the message and the ring.

Molly O'Callan came out biting her lip, a light grey cloak topping her working dress and a look of deep anxiety making her look older than her years. The note had said, '*Come out at all costs. I have to talk to you for a few minutes. Make an excuse. M.*

Her searching eyes raked Mike's withdrawn features. Acting with subtlety, she beamed for the sake of the guards, and trotted out a good excuse. 'I have to visit one or two stores. Madame's anniversary is comin' up shortly, so I have to do it secretly. The maid can manage, if I'm away for an hour or so.'

She fluttered her fingers at them, scrambled up on to the box, and breathed rather heavily until the cart had turned a corner.

Her fingers touched the back of Mike's hand. 'I'm glad you're back. You'll have heard what has happened then?'

Red passed the reins across the front of her, leaving them in Mike's hands. He then sprang to the ground and prepared to walk back into town by a different route.

Over his shoulder, he called: 'If there's any signs of a showdown with the man who disabled my cousin and me, I'd take it as a favour if you'd count me in!'

Mike grinned, and made him a promise. Molly then pressed against Mike, and he became aware that her body was shaking.

'Oh, Mike, I'm frightened. Please don't go away again!'

'There are things I have to tell you, but I'll listen first,' he offered readily.

11

Mike reached behind him in the cart and fumbled a bottle out of a wooden packing case. With the reins draped over one arm he worked with his knife to extract the cork, which eventually gave way, leaving a crumb or two in the neck. He tilted the bottle wide of the cart, dribbled away sufficient white wine to be rid of the offending impurities and then handed the bottle over to Molly.

She hesitated about not having a glass. He said: 'Drink.' She raised the bottle rather nervously. The first time, a tiny trickle of wine escaped, but when she was further encouraged, she did better.

'It is an acquired art, my dear, drinking from a bottle, especially in a moving cart.'

Presently, Molly stopped shaking and

was able to speak coherently of her fears and doubts.

'This, this Ramon. He came suddenly one day with his two *Légionnaire* assistants. He insisted that he was of the same blood as *Madame*, and I had to call her eventually. I thought he looked more like a bull-fighter than a former officer in the Foreign Legion, but the military cloak looked good on him and he had the manner born.'

Mike encouraged the two horses to get a move on. He wanted to be off the common trail and on relatively private ground rendered attractive with a small creek.

'He talked a lot in French, I suppose,' he prompted.

'Oh, yes, he did. Frenchmen have this manner about them. A lot of the things he mentioned over afternoon tea made *Madame* blush. At first it did not seem to matter, because she needed something to distract her from the worry of the old man's fatal illness. Of course a lot of what he said went over my head. I don't have your facility with the French.'

'What made *Madame* take him in, and keep him? This doesn't seem like overnight courtesy, such as *Monsieur le Marquis de Louvain* experienced. There must have been something special.'

Molly nibbled her nail, seeking inspiration. 'I know what it was. The painting! Would you believe it he had a painting of *Madame*, done by himself, so he said?'

She threw up her arms to show how big the painting was. Mike nodded and encouraged her to go on. 'So the painting had a special signal effect on *Madame*?'

'It surely did, especially as he said he had painted it from memory, havin' been in love with her some years ago. And she fell for it. She's stopped taking breakfast on her own. It looks as if he's there for good.'

'Has he been near the *Comte*, at all?'

'No, never. I don't know whether she doesn't want the old man disturbed, or whether Ramon has some reason for stayin' away from him. But so far as I know, Ramon has never been near the old man's room.'

Mike was silent for a while. Some of the things he had to bring to Molly's attention were very likely going to make her much more afraid than she was when she first appeared. In order to give her a breathing space, he talked about the eccentric *Marquis de Louvain*, and the quaint happenings on the journey through Little Springs into Texas.

On occasion, the young Texan could produce a droll way of telling a story. On this particular outing he excelled himself. Molly laughed until she cried. After a while, she knew that he was doing it on purpose, and she realised once again that this young male survivor of the Liddell family had an agile brain, as well as a cool nerve, on occasion.

Mike manoeuvred the cart to within five yards of the creek, which was about twenty yards wide and possessed a mild current at that spot. He lifted Molly to the ground, watched her take off her mocassins and put her toes in the water.

'If I had the proper clothing, I think I would bathe,' the girl confessed longingly. 'Swimmin' is one thing I miss in the service of the Beauclercs.'

'I'm goin' to have a swim, myself,' Mike informed her, 'but you can as well. Take off your things and stay down this way. I'll keep away up there. It'll do you good.'

Molly peered longingly into the distance. 'My old Irish mother used to say that if a man saw a woman's naked body it was a mortal sin. Would you agree with her?'

Mike laughed. 'Some women are neatly fashioned, it's a mortal sin to be covered up. And what if a man accidentally catches sight of a woman? It doesn't take away her beauty, or anything, does it?'

'I wouldn't know,' Molly confessed.

'I've never been through the experience. Yet.'

Mike wandered away. He stripped off behind a tree and plunged in without looking Molly's way. He had crossed the creek using a powerful overarm stroke by the time she ran in, lost her footing and hurriedly flailed the water in a graceful, but ineffective breaststroke. She engaged in a splashing fight for a time, but soon tired, being out of condition for swimming. Mike held back, diving below the surface, until she got out and leisurely dried herself behind the cart.

Her figure was superb, and he thought that she ought to have been married to some deserving male years earlier. Having towelled himself dry, he approached her with the towel firmly draped around him, and she allowed him to help dry her hair. The bathing had firmed up her body so that she looked radiant, even under the stock size drab work dress.

Mike slowly tired of drying her

tresses. He paused, breathless, gave her a brief kiss on the ear and pointed to the cart.

'Molly, I want you to get that tube and bring it over here. I'll go and grab my clothes.'

The girl nodded and moved off. Mike ran to the trees, and hurriedly manoeuvred himself into his underwear, trousers and shirt. Suddenly, she whistled. He looked up, but she was only reacting to the painting.

'Where did you get this?' she asked breathlessly.

'I brought it back from Little Springs. Found it on view in a shop window, there. What do you make of it?'

'But that's *Madame la Baronne*! I'd swear to it this painting was hanging in the house not very long ago. It's a mystery how it ever came to be in Little Springs.'

'Whereabouts was it in the house? Can you remember?'

'On the wall, in *Madame*'s bedroom, I think. I have an idea she took it down for something. The frame didn't seem to suit any more. But you must know how it came to be there. Why are you keeping me in suspense?'

'I don't know for sure, Molly. I thought you might be able to help with the explanation. Cast your mind back to the so-called burglary where nothing was missing. Don't you think it's just possible the painting might have been removed at that time before Roxy got his fatal wound?'

'I suppose it could have,' Molly replied, frowning and sitting down beside the cart. 'Wouldn't it have to be thrown out of the window, though, to disappear completely, an' reappear in a town some distance away?'

Mike knelt beside her and nodded. As he applied a match to a small cigar, he paused. 'I think Roxy might have been ordered to get it, an' when he stumbled over something, his partner outside received the painting and threw the knife which killed him.'

Molly shuddered and cupped her

face in her hands. Mike fetched the wine bottle before he put her cloak around her. The wine stopped her teeth from chattering, and he cuddled her gently as they talked.

'I — I was the only one in the room, I think, other than yourself, who heard Roxy mention a name. Ramon. Do you think this Ramon is the same person Roxy meant?'

'There are not many men in the west with a name like that,' Mike opined. 'Does he bother you, at all?'

Molly paled behind her tan and freckles. 'Yes, he does. He has a special way of lookin' at women. As if they were his prey and he was some sort of predator. You know what I mean?'

Mike nodded. Molly's voice was reduced to a whisper, as she resumed.

'One night, he caught me. Upstairs. Between rooms. He held me in a vice-like grip against the wall. I could have cried out, at first, but I hesitated, on account of the *Comte*. Then his eyes, so close to mine, seemed to turn my will to water. I'm sure he would have molested me if *Madame* herself had not come quietly up the stairs at that moment.

'He released me, and was gone in a flash.' She paused, willing away the memory. 'I suppose *Madame* is a very attractive woman, and she has a good background, and a fortune. Well, but, if this Ramon wants her, *and* her fortune, why should he be involved in the theft of her painting? To me it seems unnecessary.'

'I think he wanted to use it to captivate her. Do you not think this one is like the picture he was supposed to do of her, from memory?'

Molly studied the picture again. She had started to shake her head when she became thoughtful again.

'On the one he did, she was seated, like this. In the same pose. But she had a pale blue dress on. I thought it was funny at the time, but she had her hair piled up on her head. Usually, when she's in a day dress she brushes it all out, around her neck and shoulders.'

Mike blew twin jets of smoke from his nostrils. 'So you don't think an artist of modest talents could have used this picture to do a copy of sorts, and then disposed of it afterwards?'

'Is *that* what he did?' Molly asked breathlessly. 'I must say he's fairly good at animals. Like the little white mare, but I didn't think he was much good at humans. He did one, and painted it out again.'

She gasped, as if she had only just realised what a villain Ramon Perrier really was. Mike had never seen her with the shakes before. She cried, and wept copiously and said she was never going back. It took almost a half hour to calm her down and get her to talk reasonably about a situation which might become critical.

'You'll go back, Molly, because you're a tough little Irish woman. The thing you've done best all your life is to serve others. *Madame* is going to need you. For a while, at least, until such time as I can get some sort of proof that Ramon is a scheming villain with a past which ought to qualify him for the central character in a necktie party.'

'I — I'd rather go away with you, Michael. I could be your servant, or, anything else you wish. To me, you are security. To go back to that house is tempting providence. He'll take a lot of shifting. Why should we go on bein' lucky?'

Mike worked hard to comfort her, but it was not easy.

On the way back, Molly seemed small, inside her cloak, and his mind kept going back to the Liddell household in a far off Texas town where Molly had always seemed like part of the family, as he was growing up. He thought of his two brothers, killed in the war, and his father's slow death after it.

He had a sudden feeling that he might never see his old mother in far-off Philadelphia. It occurred to him that she might already be dead, and him not knowing, communications being as poor as they were.

The cart nearing the town brought their thoughts to a head.

'Molly, if I'm not about, you must get in touch with the local people. That is, if you think Ramon is plannin' some sort of evil. And if it comes to the crunch, you must put yourself before *Madame*. Save yourself, and I'll come back for you. The Liddells are indebted to you, and there's a bond between you and me which could always stay as affection, or turn to something else, if you wanted. Be careful, be cautious. Run away, if you have to. If you do, I'll find you, an' that's a promise.'

Somehow, she recovered her poise and her mouth — after the kissing — set in the small hard line she kept for pedlars and cheating shopkeepers.

'I'll leave a deposit for a gift in the luxury shop,' he promised.

She was so carried away, that she did not recollect for nearly a minute that she was supposed to be seeing about an anniversary gift for *la Baronne*.

'Where, or how will I contact you, Mike?' she murmured, as he put her down.

'Jock McArthur is a good friend, even if he's a noisy one. And there's Red Palin. You remember his last words before he went off? He's no coward, and his cousin will fight back when he is well again.'

'But you are goin' out of town, though?'

'I have to, Molly. I must seek for proof. Something to put him away, or at least get him away. I'll be thinking about you all the time. We'll swim again, soon. *Hasta la vista*.'

She clung to his hand like a drowning person for a few seconds longer, and then ran into the house, observed only by one of the guards, who emerged from the stable tunicless, with a soapy brush in his hand.

Mike, himself, felt distressed. At one time, he had thought the chateau the one place on earth to have the freedom of; now, he saw it as some sort of a trap for women. Possibly a death trap.

He drummed up a little anger as he returned the cart. There was no earthly use in alerting Abel Smith, the hard-faced town marshal. *He* saw the chateau as a community apart from Sundown, and no one could really blame him, as the Beauclercs had always taken care of themselves and discouraged a lot of mixing with the locals.

Smith would be secretly pleased if he knew the *Baronne* had taken in one Frenchman too many; one who was a little too difficult for her to handle, even with her money and her private guards.

Red Palin called to him from the sidewalk. Obviously, the ex-guard was curious, wanted to help. But there was little that Mike could say, at this stage, even to him.

12

The next forty-eight hours were bad for Mike Liddell's nerves. All that time, he had been in Sundown torn between two courses of action. On the one hand, he thought he ought to leave town and follow up a rather negative sort of lead which would take him on a good day's ride to Pecos Creek, one of the two towns of Sunset County located further west. On the other hand, there were considerations connected with the danger to Molly and the Beauclerc family.

He felt that his hands were tied in the second matter, inasmuch as he could not dash into the chateau, a place where he had lost face with the titled lady in charge, and make unfounded accusations against a glib, resourceful Frenchman with an interesting background and the added advantage of a distant tie by marriage.

At nine in the morning, he had a short talk with Red Palin, who had conversed with a town delivery man recently back from the chateau. Nothing seemed to have changed. The Frenchman was in evidence across the big garden situated on the northern aspect. *Madame* was out with him, calling affectionately and that was about all. Molly had waved to the tradesman from the kitchen door, and young Carmelita had run as far as the vehicle to bring a last message. It was clear that the Mexican girl was afraid of the two lounging guards at the front: afraid even to converse with them.

Mike was about to inform Red of his intention to leave town when the whole situation was transformed. A lightweight rig belonging to the chateau came up the street, pulled by a stocky roan gelding, the Beauclercs' utility work horse. Holding the reins was the shorter of the two French guards, Jacques Ribaud, and holding onto the crosswise rear seat was none other than Molly O'Callan, herself.

'Stop, here, please, *monsieur*!' Molly called.

And Mike, who was sharing a seat on the sidewalk outside the Sundown Hotel with Red, wondered where she had found her courage from.

He murmured: 'I don't know what's afoot, Red, but if you could sidetrack this little sidewinder for a bit, I might have a chance to talk privately with Molly for a while, an' that could only do good!'

'I don't like the look of him, Mike, but for you I'll give it a try. I take it we don't want to tangle with the Ramon outfit right now. Only information is required.'

Mike nodded. Molly called a greeting, and her escort roughly handed her down to the sidewalk and only then resumed the sinister expression familiar to those who had seen him on guard duty.

Red stood up quickly and touched

his hat. 'Mornin', Miss Molly. You'll have business to transact. Perhaps I can take your friend along for a drink while you are busy?'

Molly actually laughed out loud. She clapped a hand to the green headscarf which was holding back her copper-coloured tresses and hurriedly placed herself between the Frenchman and Mike. Her attention was fully on Red when she talked. She had on her grey walking-out cloak, moccasins and a simple fawn frock. Mike lowered his head as the guard took stock of him.

'Why, that surely is a nice suggestion, Red! This is *Monsieur Jacques*, and his work at the chateau sure is thirst-raisin'. He'd be more than passin' bored with the talkin' I have to do to the luxury shop man, an' an' dress-makers an' all! Why don't you take him along to the Sundowner bar? Mr. Darwin is always interestin' to talk to when you're drinkin'. Here's a dollar for the first drink. I'm sure you both deserve it.'

Red knew he was being manipulated away from Mike. He did not mind that, but he thought having to be agreeable to this vicious little *ex-legionnaire* in the presence of Bluey, who openly disliked men of that type, might prove to be difficult. Jacques Ribaud hesitated, but only for a few seconds. One thing his desert service had taught him, the slaking of the thirst was one of the great joys in life.

Flashing his gapped teeth, he called a brief, '*Au revoir,*' over his shoulder and quickly followed Red down the sidewalk and into the next entrance.

Ignoring anyone else who might be interested, Molly moved into Mike's protective arms and felt her body mildly suffused in joy.

'Is everything all right, Molly?' he whispered.

She nodded against his chest. 'So far, all's well. If anything Ramon is more arrogant, more domineering. He is certainly closer to Madeleine, *Madame*, that is. Whether that's good for her, I still don't know. But it probably means Carmelita and I will be safe for a bit longer.'

Mike eased her down on the seat. 'I'm glad you came. I was on the point of makin' a move out of town, an' I don't have anything very substantial to go on. Have you any news?'

'Not news exactly, but something that might help. I hope. Take me into the hotel dining room. It's usually deserted at this time. We have to talk, now we have the opportunity. Other chances might be few and far between.'

Over a pot of coffee, sipped slowly while they ate flap-jacks, gradually they exchanged information. 'I've done a bit of work on the telegraph. Firstly, I tried to contact my friend, the undertaker, Earl Martin. But he and his boys appear to be away from their base. That was a set-back.'

'But you must have found out something, Mike, otherwise you wouldn't be planning to leave town.'

Mike nodded and grinned. 'By the

way, that isn't my friend's real name. So he doesn't like publicity. I contacted this man who picks up messages for him in Indian Ridge. It took two or three messages before I got anywhere. Even then, it didn't amount to much. Apparently the newspaper contact in Pecos Creek, the editor of the *Creek Courier*, had what seemed like a sensational piece of news with a travelling French character involved, but it was squashed.'

'When was that?' Molly queried.

'About a month ago. It was to Pecos I was expectin' to ride. Do you have any information at all that would point me in the right direction?'

'Not information, but something which might help. Here, look at this.'

She fumbled in her shopping basket and produced from it a painting about a foot square. Mike smiled grimly when he saw it. It was a self-portrait of the infamous Ramon: head and shoulders only. Hatless, and with his crisp black hair greased and parted down the left side. The moustache was trimmed close, as he wore it always, and scarcely wider than the full, cruel mouth. There was just a suggestion of scar tissue along the angle of the jaw, left side. Mike held it closer, and frowned at it.

'This has to be Ramon, of course, but what is this mark on his jaw?'

'He has a scar there. No one has ever dared to ask about it, unless it was *Madame*, in private. I'd say someone nicked him with a knife. It doesn't look like a bullet wound to me. Tell me, will this help you in your inquiries?'

Mike shrugged. He was not over-enthusiastic. 'It might, if I find the place where he circulated before Eastville, say.'

'Eastville?' Molly murmured, between mouthfuls.

'That was where Roxy encountered him. I can't think that's the place to look, though. I wonder if I dare go ahead, start at Pecos Creek and hope for the best. What do you think?'

Molly emptied her mouth and was

about to answer, but something startled her behind Mike's back. She coughed, not having swallowed properly, and Mike hurriedly glanced over his shoulder and saw that Jacques Ribaud was back. The ex-*legionnaire*'s bulbous eyes were blood-shot. He had the look in them of a man who has been cheated.

Mike just had time to hide the self-portrait under the menu before he arrived at the table.

'So, you are Michael Liddell, the one warned to keep away! You have tricked me, *Mademoiselle*! You must keep away from this fellow. You came to town to shop, not to 'ave an assignation!'

With Ribaud's cross bandolier swinging not far from his face, Mike nevertheless kept his cool. He moved back, rose to his feet, filled his lungs and gave out with one of his gusty laughs, the sort which had females turning to examine him on occasion.

He answered in French. '*Ma vie, mon ami*, don't the French bend the rules a little when it comes to the ladies? Me, I used to work at the chateau before you did. Do I grumble because you are now in favour and I am dropped? I do not. Surely, you do not begrudge me a few words with my old friend, *l'Irlandaise*, huh?'

Mike brought his face closer, and chuckled. Ribaud hesitated. The wine and the warmth of the room tipped the balance. He relaxed, accepted the offer of good wine, and agreed to wait in the dining room another ten minutes while Mike helped Molly with essential shopping. As they sauntered thankfully towards the door, the Frenchman called over his shoulder.

They paused. Mike wondered what the outcome would be.

'What is it, *Monsieur Jacques*?'

'Shopping, an' nothing else! *Entendu*?'

Mike breathed more easily. He called that he understood, and helped Molly out into the fresh air. She had recovered the portrait from its hiding place and she handed it over for the second time. As he received it, Mike had a new idea.

He went back in, alone.

'Hey, Jacques, you and your friends must have known a lot of fine women before you came to this place. Why don't you tell me where the prettiest girls in the county are to be found, eh? I have to move on, you know.'

Ribaud toyed with his wine glass. He was watching Mike's expression in a mirror on the opposite wall. Once again, the smile temporarily took over.

'You could try Middleton. But no.'

As soon as he had uttered the name of the town, he appeared to regret it. 'No, not that. It is the wine talking. What am I thinking about? You could try Eastville, but that's not so good. Or maybe Little Springs, although there is not much talent about.'

Mike patted him on the shoulder, gesturing to the waiter and tossed down a coin to cover the wine. 'We won't be long, *mon ami*. I'll have her sitting in the rig in fifteen minutes. *Adieu*.'

Ribaud watched his reflection all the way out, but he made no attempt to stop Mike's departure. The latter rejoined Molly, fervently hoping that he hadn't set the scruffy little guard thinking about her availability.

Mike whispered: 'He may have given the game away. He mentioned Middleton, and then regretted it.'

They whispered during a hurried five minutes' visit to the luxury shop and then backtracked to the conveyance. Mike's nerves were playing him up. 'What will you do if this little jasper starts to make advances towards you?'

'I'll tell him I'm pregnant,' Molly answered promptly. 'I'm told that always cools off the over-amorous.'

She was laughing to herself as Mike handed her up to the seat. Later, when he watched them drive off from his secret lookout spot, he could still detect the twinkle in her becoming green eyes.

★ ★ ★

Middleton. A town situated half way between Indian Ridge and the Pecos river which was the western boundary of the county of Sunset. Middleton had once been called Middletown, on account of its geographical location. The actual name diminished. Somehow, the population was maintained after early attempts to raise valuable minerals had failed. However, there were few signs of great affluence and no signs of an imminent expansion.

Mike moved in after two days' punishment in the saddle. He had to use a whole lot of will power to see to the hard-ridden chestnut, but as soon as he was assured that it was in good hands and getting the right sort of treatment, he began to relax.

All the time he was eating his late afternoon meal, his eyes and ears were busy, and soon after that he commenced to put on an act calculated to draw out any special feeling for wandering Frenchmen. He had three saloons to choose from, and he started with the smallest, actually enjoying the beer.

He simulated early drunkenness, babbled away in French, told to nobody in particular that he was in town searching for an old friend, name of Ramon. Having made an impact of sorts, he staggered out and moved along to the telegraph office. There, the clerk, who was thinking about packing up for the night, sent a cryptic message to Jake Rufton, in Indian Ridge, to the effect that Mr. Martin's friend was visiting Middleton. This was just on the offchance that the Marden outfit was in the vicinity, and could be contacted.

Mike then resumed his drunken searching Frenchman act in the next saloon. His heart would have thumped, had he known that a reaction to his performance had already occurred.

13

At eight-thirty the following morning, when Mike was coming away from his café breakfast in his assumed talkative mood, a mild-mannered, self-effacing middle-aged fellow with a clerk's stoop doffed his derby hat and accosted him on the sidewalk.

'Pardon me, sir, but the word has gone around that you've been making enquiries about a missin' friend.'

Mike examined the fellow's face eagerly. He touched his own hat, nodded and waited.

'If you'll be so good as to accompany me, I know of someone who is very keen to talk with you.'

The Texan, who couldn't think of a better hour of the day for a sudden development in his enquiries, fell into step beside the clerk and arrived outside a branch of the West Sunset

Banking Company in a very few minutes. He was ushered in ahead of the employee, who indicated a padded seat and asked him to wait.

Early customers gave him the once-over as they queued at the counter and made their transactions. The messenger came back from the private room, minus his hat, and indicated that a Mr. Charlton Wagner, no less a personage than the president, was ready to interview him right away.

The private room was nicely done out. A picture of the originator who could have been the current president's father gave the wall behind the main desk a touch of class. Charlton Wagner hurriedly signed a couple of forms, the slightly wrinkled skin around his left eye twitching occasionally under the pressure of a thin-rimmed monocle.

While Mike's eyes and the pen were still busy, the president remarked in a cultured voice. 'I'm afraid you have the advantage of me, sir. I'm Charlton

Wagner, as you know. I don't know your name.'

Mike juggled easily with his hat, nodded and smiled. 'That's easily remedied, Mr. Wagner. I'm Mike Liddell. Michael Bonnard Liddell, if you want it in full. Raised in Texas, mostly, and you might say a traveller of sorts, by profession.'

The president's pen slowed perceptibly as his visitor presented a word picture of himself. Wagner lowered his pen, screwed himself rather more comfortably into his green-leather padded swivel chair, and leaned over his bent arms.

'Yes, I see. You were heard to ask after a travelling French gentleman, Mr. Liddell. Now me, I have an excellent memory for faces, but years have made it difficult in remembering names. Do you, perhaps, have a photo or a portrait of your missing friend? I take it he is missing?'

Mike shrugged and smiled, answering evasively. 'I do have a portrait, as it happens, Mr. Wagner. If you've ever seen Ramon at all, you'll know him by this.'

He dipped inside his smooth black leather hanging vest and brought out the portrait, which was in an envelope tailored to its size. Wagner grunted, nodded, took the envelope and removed the contents. As he did so, Mike took the opportunity to study the older man.

Wagner was around sixty years of age. A little over the average in height and a few pounds over weight. His grey hair had receded a lot, and what was left of it was creamed and brushed straight back. He had the standard professional person's office clothing on him: a stiff collar, black tie, black jacket and grey trousers. There was a keenness in his brown eyes which belied his years. He talked like a man with a disciplined mind, and yet there was something else behind the everyday façade of his manners.

Mike wondered if he was a basically sad man.

Charlton clicked his tongue. 'This man was around these parts a few weeks back. I think I'm in a position to do you a favour. If you want to hear more about him, I can put you in touch with someone who knows more.'

'When is the contact likely to be?' Mike asked, on the edge of his chair.

Wagner sniffed and allowed his monocle to drop. 'It'll be a short way out of town. Possibly this afternoon. Now, why don't you go back to your hotel and wait? I'll send a messenger for you when the meeting is set up. Someone who can guide you to the cabin.'

Mike found himself nodding automatically. An invitation to a cabin, well out of town. He had a curious feeling that history might once again be about to repeat itself. That other time had been a near thing: when he was ambushed, and had to shoot his would-be assassin. His pulse registered an uneven beat.

'All right, Mr. Wagner, we'll do it

your way. I can't rightly think why you're putting yourself to all this trouble, on my behalf.'

The two men rose together, shook hands, and Mike left. Wagner slumped in his chair with a faraway look in his eyes, breathing on his monocle and absently polishing it on a large white handkerchief.

* * *

No one came near Mike, who was passing most of his waiting time in the foyer of the hotel. The whole of the afternoon went by, and he took to pacing the carpet which annoyed the manager who was thinking in terms of wear and tear.

One occasion was almost critical. The manager came and stood in front of him to dissuade him. Mike made an effort, and chose that time to slip out as far as the bank. There were a few strollers on the sidewalk, but he found the bank closed up for the day, and nobody seemed to want to show him the way to the banker's private house.

It was all very frustrating. He took a meal in the dining room, and attracted a lot of attention when a poker-faced individual with the skin pigment of an Indian came and stood in the doorway and stared at him.

The man had on a blue felt hat, round and flat-crowned. Some people seemed to resent his presence but no one insisted on his being ejected, which suggested to Mike that he was well known in the town.

Mike grabbed the waiter, who cursed briefly as he juggled with a plate of soup and suggested that Johnnie Two-Feathers often acted as a guide. That was the end of Mike's appetite, and he rose to his feet, glowered at the disturbed guests and moved out of the room to question the impassive one.

Two-Feathers blinked at him and led the way into the street. He was not much over five feet in height. His black hair was cut to a forehead fringe and snipped off in a straight line all the way round his head just below the ears. He wore a blue buttoned shirt, denim trousers and a dark leather jacket.

Mike stood between the messenger and his pinto horse and asked a series of questions, to which he received answers in the form of positive nods. Gradually, he elicited the information that Johnnie was acting for Mr. Wagner, the bank president, that he was to take Mike on a journey out of town, right away. And a few other details.

Fretting with frustration, Mike then raced off to the livery and ran out the chestnut, waiting for the Indian to come up with him on the plodding two-tone horse.

The route out of town was first westward, and then a change of direction made it approximately north-westward. The hour was between eight and nine in the evening when they set off. Mike found himself brooding over that earlier ambush when Ringo Marden had sought to eliminate him because he was seeking information about the murdered Richard Beauclerc. On that occasion, someone had slipped into a hotel room and pinned a note to the clothing of the late Roxy Barlow, actually scratching his skin at the same time.

Being taken along by a seemingly mindless Indian certainly was a change, if he was really heading into trouble. But would a thoroughly respectable bank president be a party to taking an enquiry agent out into the wilds to be ambushed?

Experience was fast teaching Mike that you never could tell. All kinds of extremely respectable citizens had problems, and things they didn't want others to know about.

Mike felt his nerves. In the sky the setting sun moved with a maddening slowness towards the extinguishing western horizon. He moved up with Johnnie Two-Feathers and protested at the slowness of the pace, but that got him nowhere. Clearly, the placid Indian had his orders. Contact was to be made after nightfall.

Mike dropped back a yard or so, and groaned. He tried to think of the days before he became embroiled with the Beauclercs and their doings and those earlier memories seemed blurred, insignificant and of another world. He gave up trying after a while, and focused on more recent events. It was easy, for instance, to imagine Molly tucked up in her bed with the curtains open and an odd shaft of moonlight illuminating the picture of her mother hanging on the wall. And *Madame*. She used to retire early and read a book, with a small pair of reading spectacles on her nose and a tiny expensive lamp hanging low over the bed-head. The vision was clear, but it became obscure again as he reasoned that she might be no longer alone.

'How much longer, Two-Feathers?'

The Indian shrugged elegantly and flipped his reins over the pinto's head. They moved through a stand of timber and when they emerged again the sky was perceptibly darker. Mike thought morosely that they might not have a lot further to go. The scene was set, if there was going to be any bush-whacking or the like.

Five minutes later, Johnnie waited for him and pointed the way off-trail on the north side. They negotiated a short claustrophobic passage between over-hanging walls of rock and finally emerged into the upper slopes of a secluded valley.

There was a light breeze, which gently sighed through scattered stands of pine and deciduous trees. In the expiring glow of sunset there was a distant reflection on water and, not so far away, the eerie glow of a turned-down lamp in a low-lying dwelling.

'Is that the place?' Mike enquired hoarsely.

'Yes, that is it,' the Indian replied, unexpectedly.

Sighing with relief, Mike increased the pace of the sweating chestnut and moved slightly into the lead. If this was to be an ambush of any sort, the set-up was at least different. The lamp confirmed that someone was on the premises, and there was a distant mouthing of animals from beyond the building. A parked gig had its shafts pointing upwards. The smell of wood smoke emanated from a stove pipe.

Even the tired horses seemed to be more than a little interested during the run-in over the last fifty yards. Mike kept an eye on his companion, but the Indian was as self-contained as he had been ever since the first meeting.

As they dismounted, Mike thought the lamplight might have increased. Nothing changed, however, and he found himself walking up to the building with curiosity and excitement mounting in him at every step. He knocked and tried the door, which opened readily enough. A pleasant lived-in aroma assailed his nostrils. He took off his hat, stepped inside and looked around for signs of life. Johnnie Two-Feathers was still outside.

In the shadowy glow from the lamp, he could see a two-tier bunk up against the wall, directly opposite. Many of the isolated cabins he had visited had no floor, other than beaten earth. This one had a wooden floor, solid enough to take any amount of weight without creaking. It also had strips of thin carpet in places. One of these strips started at the doorway and went all the way across the shack and under the lower of the two bunks opposite.

He was standing on one end of it. His gaze followed it to the other end, where he noticed that the two bunks were occupied. Each held the bulky blanketed figure of — presumably — a man. The sleepers both had their heads to the wall, facing away from him.

The surprise, therefore, was complete when the carpet on which he was standing suddenly jerked away from him and he fell heavily on his back, just inside the door, which had closed. His assailants came from either side. A hard, working man's fist hit him hard on the right side of his jaw. He was aware of tobacco-tainted breathe as he lost balance again, and somersaulted away from the punch.

Somewhere in the building, a rocking chair creaked eerily. Mike's back met a booted leg as he strove to come to his feet. Groping hands relieved him of knife and revolver before the knee propelled him forward again. He slipped a punch, mainly by instinct and wrestled his first attacker aside. At the same time, the man from the lower bunk slid easily to his feet and reached up to the lamp.

A fist swung up from his first assailant and landed with only half its original force. Nevertheless, it landed heavily on Mike's nose and mouth and knocked some of the breath out of him. Between them, they had his legs from underneath him, but he held onto the other wrestler's belt and was about to throw him when he got his breath back.

'Hold it!' he yelled. 'I don't know who you think I am, but I'd say you have the wrong man!'

There was a brief hesitation. The man who should have been thrown sank back on his legs. The man at the lamp assumed command.

'All right, back off, boys! I've got him covered!'

14

Three revolvers clicked in all: two at ground level and the third up in the open-ended loft, where the rocking chair sound had come from. The man in the rocker rose to his feet at the same time as Mike did.

The young Texan's mind was a tumbling mass of conflicting emotions as he recognised the man by the lamp, and then — with equal facility — his two attackers. He gently rubbed his mouth and nose and came away with a smear of blood. Rusty Bayer picked up the Colt and dagger from the floor and loosely tossed them on to the hardwood table. He was still chewing on a small plug of tobacco.

Rusty's brother, Sam, who had first removed the weapons, massaged the back of his neck and looked mildly embarrassed.

Mike pointed a finger at the tall man below the lamp.

'Earl Marden, of all people. Bein' called to remote cabins by the Mardens is gettin' to be the story of my life. Hell an' tarnation, Earl, I've been tryin' to get in touch with you for days, an' here you are settin' up an ambush for *me*! Just when I'm thinkin' I'm makin' progress!'

Earl said: 'I'm sorry, Mike. Like you said, it looks as if there's been a mistake.'

The former outlaw smoothly holstered his weapon and gestured to the others to relax. There was a steady trickle of blood from Mike's nose, but it did not show up much on his red bandanna.

On the upper bunk, Charlton Wagner, the bank president was seated: fully dressed in unaccustomed trail rider's clothes. He sounded nervous, nonplussed, as he worked his monocle into his eye. 'Well, that's the fellow, Earl, I assure you. A pity, I suppose, his name got forgotten in the excitement. But he did express a firm interest in the galoot we're after. He called him Ramon like he'd known him all his life, and that seemed to take away all doubts. I apologise, if apology is needed.'

Mike nodded. Before he spoke again, there was a comment from the loft. 'I always said you spent too much time in figurin' an' looking into ledgers to do anything worthwhile in any form of skullduggery.'

The old man from the rocker started to come down a rough loft ladder, which creaked under his weight. He was older than the banker by a few years, as his piping voice suggested. He wore a soft grey felt hat with a rolled-up narrow brim and a baggy, shiny well-worn grey suit. Arriving at the bottom, he clipped pince nez to his bulbous nose and closely examined the latest arrival.

'Oh, this is my brother, er, Mike. He's a medical doctor, an' more or less retired these days,' the banker explained.

'Not so far retired that he would hesitate to shoot a stranger,' Mike remarked, as he took a seat on a bench beside the table.

Earl's thundering low laugh filled the building. He reached a bottle of whisky off a shelf and poured for all, setting up Mike's drink first. The rest all took seats and waited for him to drink.

Earl started the discussion. 'What's your interest in this French hombre, Ramon, Mike?'

Mike let the fiery liquid trickle down his throat before he answered the question which affected all his listeners.

'He's established himself in the Chateau Beauclerc like he's there to stay forever. *Madame la Baronne* thinks he's God's gift to women. Molly O'Callan goes in fear of being attacked by him. Me, I think he's the worst kind of villain, a menace to society. I believe he killed my old buddy, Roxy Barlow, with that knife. A throw into the throat. On Beauclerc property. Only I can't prove it. So, I was seekin' to drum up evidence of some earlier misdeed, in an effort to get rid of him for good.'

Earl said: 'I'm sorry about your partner, Barlow, although I thought he was a threat to my security, Mike. However, you may have come to the right place to get something done about the Frenchman, Ramon.'

Mike reflected that there were not many men in the west who could boast they had received Earl Marden's apologies twice within a few minutes. In the meantime, the tetchy old doctor blinked through and over his spectacles at his younger brother, stuck an unlit pipe in his mouth and finally unwrapped another black-handled dagger from its protecting cover, a large handkerchief. Side by side, the two daggers were clearly two of a set of identical weapons.

Mike felt he might guess at some of the coming revelations.

'Did Ramon Perrier use that knife, doctor, on someone you know?'

Wagner, the banker, dropped his head and almost choked on suppressed grief. The doctor waited for him to signify that he should go on.

'Maybe a couple of months back, or something like that. I ain't all that good any more over times and dates, this handsome Frenchman appeared in Middleton fresh out of nowhere. He caused a bit of a sensation. Showed a bit of style an' class round about the time when we were havin' a barn dance, and a bit later a smart weddin' for the mayor's daughter.

'I have to tell you, though it hurts my brother, that his wife, Eleonora, took a sudden liking to this Ramon. Charlton met his wife, who was only thirty years of age when she died, on a visit to San Francisco. He was indulgent towards her, because he loved her dearly and because she needed to let her hair down now and again, have a good time with folks her own age.

'Unfortunately, the innocent affair with Ramon ... Ramon Perrier, if that's his proper name, got out of hand. He took her for rides, sometimes on horseback, sometimes in a surrey. And Eleonora was captivated by him.'

The banker coughed to clear his throat. 'Sam will you have the goodness to get on with the story? You always were a good talker, but this isn't the time to excel yourself. Now, is it?'

'Sorry, Charlie. I'll cut it down some. Eleonora was so far misguided as to lay her hands on ten thousand dollars of the bank funds and pass them over to Ramon. Apparently, she thought he was going to elope with her. However, he had other ideas. When she accidentally found out he planned to go without her, there was a quarrel.

'We think he threw this knife at her, just at the time when she was about to throw back her head and denounce him, in a loud voice. She was found, after he had gone, with the knife buried to the hilt in her breast. Which explains why my brother, a hard-working, shrewd, utterly honest businessman, would sink to murder this instant if Perrier happened to be present.'

Mike cleared his throat. 'I regret the hurt, Mr. Wagner, but I think I had to know your end of the story. I don't think I've heard all of it, yet, however.'

The big masculine hand of Earl Marden came down over that of the doctor, who shrugged and permitted him to finish off the tale.

'Rightly, or wrongly, Mike, Charlie here, decided that he didn't want a lot of harrowing county-wide publicity about his deceased wife's affair with a wandering philanderer, culminating in robbery and murder. So Sam, there, signed a death certificate of sorts, and folks were allowed publicly to believe that poor Eleonora had taken her own life on account of some fatal illness which the family had kept to themselves.

'I owed Sam Wagner a few favours from the days when my boys were on the run and needed patchin' up without publicity, so I chipped in and helped with the funeral. Furthermore, I offered to help the Wagner brothers in any way

I could to get after this Perrier character and make him pay in the rather unorthodox methods occasionally used among western gentry. So, you see how things stand?'

Mike nodded and fished in his pocket for a cigar. He found three, and tipped the two spare ones on the table for anyone who fancied a smoke. Noticeably, Earl and his boys withheld in favour of the veteran Wagner brothers.

'If it wasn't so painful,' Mike opined, 'this would be an interestin' situation. As far as Perrier is concerned, it would be very difficult to bring a charge against him concerning the money, and even more difficult on the count of murder, seein' as how people believe Mrs. Wagner took her own life. Am I right so far?'

'You're right,' the banker assured him. 'Which is why our mutual friend, Earl, suggested unorthodox methods. Mike, I am fairly rich and extremely bitter. If you want money for eliminating this Perrier, I will provide it. I don't need to know what means you use. But as you seem to be working along the same lines as we are I'd like you to have a hand, a profitable hand, if you like, in Perrier's future.'

Mike removed his cigar from his mouth. 'Thank you for your offer, Mr. Wagner, but I won't take money for this one. There'll have to be a showdown of some sort, and I'll need help because Perrier has a couple of vicious-looking sidekicks. Murderers both, I'd say, and most likely well versed in many ways of killing, since they have the stamp of the Foreign Legion upon them.'

'Are you askin for me an' my boys, Mike?' Marden asked lightly.

Mike smiled for the first time since he entered that fateful shack. 'I don't think I could manage without your help, and there's no outfit I'd rather have backin' me.'

'That bein' so, me an' the boys will make ourselves available to you right away. How do you see the near future?'

Mike filled in a few details about the

set-up at the chateau and also mentioned about the *Comte*'s imminent death.

Earl, acting as chairman, made a pronouncement. 'Gentlemen, I think we can safely say that this little episode which might have gone sour on us, turned out for the best. I seem to smell urgency, in the revelations of our friend, Mike Liddell. Vengeance is never a pleasant thing, but if we wait too long, another innocent woman or women, may pay the penalty.

'I vote we all take a few hours' sleep. After that, Mike an' my outfit will high-tail it for Sundown to bring this unfortunate business to a climax. What do you say?'

Everyone present was in favour. 'Charlie' Wagner had something to add. 'Gents, I'm sure you'll do us all proud, but as for me, I can't go back to my comfortable banking job until this issue is settled. I'll be comin' along to Sundown maybe just a little bit slower than some of you.

'Maybe I can be of help. I have a few influential friends in the town, and I'd be glad to talk to that titled lady about my own losses if it would help to keep her out of trouble.'

Mike was whistling absently as he spread out his blankets for a shake-down. Asked if there was anything special troubling him by Sam Bayer, he remarked: 'I was just thinkin' an' hopin' that none of us present get in the way of thrown knives, metal balls and the South American bolas. Friend Perrier is an expert with all these unusual items, as well as with conventional weapons such as the Colt.'

The lower bunk creaked as Earl Marden lowered himself into it.

'Would you say he was strong on honour, Mike? The sort of fellow who might end things with a duel?'

'I wouldn't know, amigo,' Mike replied, as he threw his cigar butt into the stove. 'One thing I would like to do for our Ramon an' that is to return his knife, or knives.'

This bit of wishful thinking sent them all between the blankets in a thoughtful mood. There was no further discussion, and no one needed any explanation of the Texan's intentions.

15

Mike Liddell and Johnnie Two-Feathers were the first to ride out from the isolated shack and head back to Middleton. Marden and his boys were stirring by the time they reached the top of the valley and the Wagner brothers, who had not slept particularly well, were not difficult to rouse.

The Indian guide actually gave out with three pieces of information on the way back into town and clearly he had been primed by his employer, Charlton Wagner, to give Liddell any sort of help which he might need.

Mike turned over the chestnut to the Indian, who was supposed to take it to the stable for grooming while he — Mike — partook of breakfast and fortified himself for the long ride back. The young Texan read a paper over the interval while his food was being cooked and his mind was elsewhere when the outline of a persistent man appeared through the curtains of the restaurant.

Two-Feathers was asked to move indoors. He did so reluctantly feeling out of place in a white American café, but he had with him a written note from the telegraph office addressed to M. Liddell Esq., and that assignment gave him the courage he needed to brave the sarcastic tongues of any who thought Indians should use a separate establishment.

However, no one queried Johnnie's presence, and Mike was able to read the message in peace and come to a decision about it.

It read: *Mike. Old man died early this morning. Come back with all speed. Love. Molly.*

With an effort, he managed to get Johnnie to sit at his table and drink coffee. While Two-Feathers slaked his thirst, Mike wrote two notes. One brief and to the point, addressed to Miss

Molly O'Callan at the Chateau Beauclerc, intimating that he had received his telegraph message and was on his way. The other was addressed to either Mr. Earl Martin, or Mr. Charlton Wagner, and the purport of the message was that *Monsieur le Comte*'s death had speeded things up, and that anyone headed for Sundown ought to get there with the least possible delay.

'Johnnie, I want you to take these two to the telegraph office. This one to be sent as a message, and the other to be kept for Mr. Wagner, the banker, or Mr. Martin, the undertaker. Got that?'

Johnnie smiled. 'Anything else, *Senor* Mike?'

'Yes, I have to ride like the wind, all the way to Sundown to attend a funeral and stop a lot of trouble. My horse is fit, but tired. I need to borrow one, straight away. Mr. Wagner will pay the expenses of anything like that. He has said so.'

'I will see to it,' Johnnie promised. He stood up, leaving half a mug of coffee, and left Mike to his thoughts.

The latter had a feeling that the present troubles of the Beauclercs were about to come to a head. The death of *Monsieur le Comte* meant that *Madame* was in sole control of the chateau and the family fortune, and that anyone who managed to marry her was in a position to scoop the lot. What a tempting situation that was for a fellow with Perrier's motivation.

Mike was pacing the sidewalk smoking a cigar when Johnnie came back down the street leading a frisky palomino gelding of about three years. He led it up to the hitch rail and at once set about removing the saddle and blanket from the chestnut, which he also had with him. He explained that the ostler had already replaced the horse jewelry after doing a makeshift grooming. The pinto had also had the same treatment.

Something about the Indian's manner made Mike think that Johnnie had misinterpreted his instructions.

'You have seen the telegraph clerk?'

Johnnie nodded. 'My brother stays with him, with the message. Me, I go with you. You may need help.'

Mike thought about a display of anger, but then he gave in. He accepted Johnnie's company and within five minutes they were headed out of town and looking for the shortest possible route to Sundown. Half a mile out of town, they encountered a family on a conestoga, and the owner assured them that there was no quicker way to Sundown than through Pecos. He also enquired if the led chestnut was for sale, and received a short answer.

The three horses, therefore, and the two riders manoeuvred themselves back onto the main Pecos trail and systematically began to knock back the miles. Mike was actually dozing in the saddle when they entered Pecos early in the afternoon. He was glad of the Indian's company at that time. They both spent a few minutes under a pump and drank some tepid beer before pushing on again, resisting the temptation to take a siesta.

The glowering sun, however, began to have its effect again and between two and three o'clock the faint but attractive sounds of running water not far from the heat-shimmering atmosphere over the trail undermined Mike's resolve to keep going at all costs. He allowed the impassive Johnnie to overtake him and admitted that he wanted to stretch out on the ground beside the stream and rest, perhaps just for one hour.

'Is good,' the Indian commented. 'You arrive Sundown very tired, no shoot straight. Hand an' eye not work good in showdown.'

Mike accepted this statement without comment and the two of them sought a pleasing stretch near the stream masked from the trail by a stand of stunted oak trees. There was trouble between the two of them later because Johnnie allowed Mike to sleep for nearer three hours than one, and a good deal of the remaining daylight was wasted.

Eventually, they entered the town of Sundown during the dark hours and from the north. The first item of information came through observation. There were no guards mounted at the front of the house. Two lamps were lit at a low illumination, and a wreath of red flowers and green foliage hung on a panel of the front door.

The still atmosphere of the usually awe-inspiring building had them talking in whispers. Mike murmured: 'Johnnie, I want you to take all three horses across the avenue and peg them out on that land the other side of the hedge. At daylight the action will start. Me, I goin' in, one way or another. You, I'd like you to camp out with the horses and be ready for any emergency. Also watch out for Mr. Martin. Understood?'

'*Comprendo, Senor Mike.*'

Johnnie was grinning as he ran the horses out of sight and prepared for a fireless camp. Mike hurled small stones, one at a time, against the high window of the butler's room, until the old man lit a lamp and came down to the second entrance and opened the door.

Joseph looked cold and troubled in his long night shirt, but he was willing to get himself into trouble by admitting Mike, as soon as he knew who it was. Only three or four sentences were exchanged before Mike bedded down in a store room adjacent to the kitchen to sleep away the hours until daylight.

There was cold food in plenty around him. He did not lack blankets, and he knew that this far the burial had not taken place.

★ ★ ★

About four in the morning, Molly, who could not sleep, catfooted down to the kitchen, found a shortage of coffee, and promptly fell over Mike's outstretched form in the store room. He recovered first, and clutched her to him, marvelling at the softness of her body, lacking the trappings of day wear and only protected by a flimsy nightdress and her grey cloak.

His hand was over her mouth to prevent a scream, and she pounded his chest in relief, as soon as she realised who it was in the semi-darkness. 'Sure, an' begorrah, me lad, you'll give some innocent woman the heart failure turnin' up unexpected like this in the middle of the night. Who let you in? Oh, don't answer that. As if I cared.'

On the under side, Mike shook with laughter, and held on tightly, all the time trying to plant a kiss on the mobile lips which continued to evade him.

'Will you stop tryin' to make a sinful woman of me, an' there bein' a priest in the house, an' all. Let me up, Michael Liddell, or I'll holler the house down, so help me.'

Very slowly, Mike released her. She pulled back a little way. Then bent over and kissed him warmly, and only when his arms started to work again did she grow difficult and get to her feet. In the kitchen, they sat opposite one another, and sipped the coffee. Only gradually did the joy of meeting go out of them.

'Thank you for comin', Mike. I guess you've been ridin' all night. And the two of us cavorting like a couple of kids under the room where the *Comte* lies dead.'

'You were sayin' about a priest, Molly,' Mike prompted, as he washed his hands and face at the sink.

'He came from a rather more saintly town than this, over the Texas border. Reckons he's been on the way for days. Only arrived half a day ago. *Madame* an' Ramon, they've spent hours in his company already. The funeral is due at two o'clock this afternoon. Service in the house, burial you know where in the gardens.'

'Any talk of a wedding?'

'Oh, yes. Things are movin' all right. The priest thinks it would be better if they waited forty-eight hours after the burial. *La Baronne* is keen all right. She can't wait a week or two to round up a few suitable families to take part in the proceedings. I've got a feelin' that will suit the fellow she's marryin' too.'

'You still think he's on the make?' Mike queried.

'Yes, at one time I thought he might be an imposter, but Madame says she's seen a birthmark on his body which makes it certain that he is who he says he is. Tell me, Mike, are you goin' to be able to stop the wedding, or have him removed, or something?'

Mike shrugged. 'I've found out about his last involvement with a woman. In Middleton. Almost certainly, he murdered her, took off with funds from her husband's bank, having deceived her into thinking he was eloping with her.'

Molly leaned towards Mike, fascinated by his revelations. She gripped his hands and gave him so much attention that he found it hard to keep his mind on the events since he had seen her last. When he started to talk with difficulty, she spirited him away to the downstairs bathroom with its adjoining dressing room, and locked him in.

His orders were to rest, until the whole house stirred. After that he was to take a bath and sharpen himself up. Food would be smuggled in, and he would be released shortly before the hour of the burial. Which was more or less what happened.

★　★　★

Father Francesco, a tall lean balding priest in his late forties, came down the avenue from the north in his smart two-horse surrey half an hour before the burial was due to take place. He had insisted on going away privately for a little exercise and a change of scene before he officiated at the burial. As a result, his white cassock had acquired a certain amount of trail dust, and a slight film of perspiration had come between his high bald crown and the small skullcap which protected it.

He was well to do, and enjoyed the

confidence of the wealthy, some of whom lived many miles away from his parish. His own background was Italian, but he was fascinated by the Beauclerc lineage; by a rich, wealthy and influential family which had nevertheless put down its roots in this backwater of New Mexico territory and seemed likely to stay there.

For a time, he was so immersed in his own thoughts, that he did not notice the approach of others from out of town, arriving behind him. Earl Marden and his boys slowed up when they saw the priest, and Father Francesco had time to park his surrey in a small lay-by off the east side of the avenue, and make his way leisurely across the gardens to the house without noticing the horse riders at all.

A Mexican gardener hurried across the gardens and made sure that the brake was on before slipping nose bags on the horses' heads, and slackening their harness. As soon as the priest had disappeared indoors, Johnnie

Two-Feathers attracted the attention of the trio of riders, who pulled off the avenue and joined him.

In some towns, the Bayers resorted to disguise of all sorts, but on this occasion it was not thought to be necessary. All they did behind the screening hedge was to freshen up a little and put on the dark clothes they habitually used when performing at a burial. Their long dark coats discreetly hid their guns and belts as they crossed the avenue, and Earl himself walked with the unmistakable tread of a man with weapons at his hips.

Ribaud and Braun, the guards appeared almost at the same time, and looked surprised when the undertaking outfit moved towards the house with measured tread. These two were washed, well shaven and their clothes nicely brushed, and yet they looked the same as always, ex-professional soldiers still living by the gun. The stocky Jacques discarded a pungent cigarette butt and stepped towards Earl with his hands fondling his bandolier and belt.

'Gentlemen, you should know by the wreath there is death in this house. No one must approach. All right?'

'I know there is death in this house because I am by profession an undertaker. I was sent for as soon as *Monsieur le Comte* was taken ill. We are a little short of time. If you will step out of the way?'

Ribaud glanced at Braun, who hesitated. The former said: 'But we were to carry the coffin, so I thought. *Monsieur Ramon* — '

'In those clothes? You are misinformed, my man.'

Earl casually shifted the hang of his black frockcoat and revealed his formidable side weapons. At exactly the same time, the Bayers did the same. It was all the intimation needed by the ex-*legionnaires* who gave ground, and cautiously withdrew round the side of the house to watch developments.

Joseph appeared. Ramon jerked him out of the way in a threatening gesture.

'What do you want?' he began, in his usual blustering manner.

'The head of the house, my little man,' Earl replied, in a voice which carried easily. 'Have the kindness to ask *Madame la Baronne* to step this way. I can assure you we are acquainted.'

Ramon hesitated for a few seconds. Madeleine appeared.

Earl doffed his hat, and smiled reassuringly. 'I am sorry we were late, *Madame*, but we are ready now. You won't need the two foreign gentlemen to carry the casket. If you'll be so kind as to admit us.'

La Baronne usually only reacted to men of powerful personality. There was never any doubt about Earl Marden's magnetism when he embarked upon an important course of action. The entry occurred smoothly, and Ramon, the intruder, was left wondering why his men had backed down in the first place. However, Ramon was nothing, if not an opportunist, and he bided his time, confident that all would go his way when the interment was over and the undertaker's men had withdrawn.

The funeral service started promptly at two p.m. Father Francesco did a tasteful professional job, being liberal with his incense and facile with his oration. Some fifteen minutes later, the Bayers shouldered the coffin, cautiously made their way out by the front door and lined up at the side of the house, behind Earl.

Ramon, wearing his adopted dark toreador-type outfit, followed close behind supporting *Madame la Baronne*, who was suitably dressed for the occasion in an expensive black dress, clinging above the waist and wide in the skirt. Her hat added to her dignity, and a thin grey veil hid her features.

There was a surprise as the servants came out from another door. Mike was there, resplendent in a white shirt with a black string tie and a black armband. He averted his face from the chief mourner and made a great show of taking Molly's arm as she slipped into place in a simple becoming black dress.

The priest took his place, and Joseph and Carmelita emerged last, both suitably attired. There was tension among the members of the short procession but no one allowed it to spoil the solemnity of the occasion. In the depths of the ornate garden, the priest behaved as though inspired, and soon it was time to sprinkle soil into the grave and lay the wreaths of flowers in place. The two veteran Mexican gardeners did their little bit. The priest moved away first. *Madame* and her escort then followed. Earl and his boys draped themselves about the burial plot like statues, and the other mourners moved away.

In a low part of the garden, there were seats on either side of a paved path, secluded by high neatly trimmed hedges. *Madame* and Ramon boldly took a seat on one side, while Mike and Molly took one opposite.

Madame stripped off her veil and hat as Ramon bared his head. Opposite them, Mike and Molly casually did the same. Ramon gestured in Mike's direction, using his fingers like a lord calling a waiter.

In French, he said: 'And this, this interloper, *Madeleine*, tell me who he is before I have him thrown out!'

Mike was without his customary leather hanging vest. He allowed Ramon, who was apparently weaponless, to view his holstered Colt and one of his knives, behind the hip on the other side. He then produced a small cigar, lighted it and smiled casually at Molly, who responded.

'This,' *Madame* began, her sarcasm born out of a feeling that she had been outmanoeuvred, 'is a certain *Michael Bonnard Liddell*. A former drifter whom I employed some time ago, and who has now inserted himself unknown to me into my household and the lives of my staff!'

Mike blew smoke across the intervening ground. He spoke up for himself, in French. '*Madame*, perhaps it is you who have allowed yourself to be distracted. You who are not up-to-date. For your information I have never ceased to work in the best interests of *la famille* Beauclerc. *Monsieur le Comte* approved of my latest efforts.'

Madeleine fumed, a becoming pink blush suffused her neck and face. Ramon noticed the Beauclerc ring on Mike's finger and the two knives with the black handles which he ostentatiously brought into view.

'Furthermore, there are things you must be told, right away before you contemplate using the priest again,' Mike added.

Madeleine, who had never been so affronted in her life, turned to her latest escort, expecting him to leap up and suggest a duel, or something of the sort. To her great surprise, Ramon, although he was much ruffled, suggested that they should all go indoors.

There was tension in the smaller of the two lounges. *Madeleine* seated herself at one end of a low cream upholstered settee. Ramon cautiously seated himself at the other end. Mike took an upright chair, so that his two hands and arms would not be encumbered if he had to make a swift move.

Mike and Ramon both knew that the latter's discarded gun and knife belt were reclining on a magnificent antique chest of drawers with gently curved legs, against one wall. *Madeleine* was seated nearest to it. Molly dropped into her usual role, pouring wine from a decanter into glasses and carrying it to the assembled three people. *La Baronne* first, of course, and at the same time *Madame* received the rolled up canvas of herself which Mike had found and bought in Little Springs.

She took a sip of her wine, grounded the glass on a small table, unrolled the painting and gasped. 'Where did you get this, Molly?' *Madeleine*'s eyes were on Mike, as she spoke, but she was in no mood to ask him questions.

'Mike found it in a shop, on his travels, *Madame*. He thought you might like it back, seein' it had been stolen from your bedroom by the man who died there, an' passed on to his partner.'

La Baronne smiled at Ramon and got a frosty response. 'I didn't notice the theft. Why would anyone want to steal my portrait?'

Mike took his glass, smiled reassuringly at Molly, and answered. 'In order to use it. The painter wanted to copy your stance and other details, so he had Roxy Barlow steal it.'

Perrier emptied his glass in one long swallow. 'You want to hear more of these remarkable insinuations, *ma cherie*?'

'Have you ever seen a knife like this?' Mike asked, holding out one of the Perrier pair so that she could see it closely.

Madeleine studied it and shrunk away from it. Ramon was very tense, but he was still listening. 'This is the one that came out of Roxy's death wound, it is just like the one in that belt over there. I have another one which came out of the bosom of a beautiful woman who thought she was in love with Ramon Perrier. He killed her as he did Roxy Barlow with a thrown knife.'

'That's enough,' Perrier protested. 'All these things you say are monstrous. They are unfounded. You, I think, are jealous of the love Madeleine feels for me. But you must be silenced . . . '

He was putting on a good performance, but *la Baronne* needed to know more.

'If you are saying these things to humiliate me, *Michel*, I wish you wouldn't.' She turned to Ramon 'Did you know this woman he speaks of?'

He seated himself again, this time considerably nearer to *la Baronne*. Obviously, he was torn between two courses of action. One was to preserve his image with Madame at all costs, and the other was to upstage this loquacious Texan and wipe him out at the earliest possible moment. Moreover, Perrier knew that he had often ruined his own chances of fortune by precipitate action. Even now, he was some little distance from his revolver and knife, and the Texan was in a good position for a fast move.

Ramon looked up, gave a wry smile to all of them. Molly, whose heart was thumping with fear, hovered in the background and wondered if this was the prelude to violent action. Ramon, however, became wistful as he turned his head rather quizzically in the direction of *la Baronne*.

'There was a woman. I have to admit it. There have been others. I seem to have a fatal charm. I attract them.'

Mike, who had been patiently working on the Frenchman's nerves, knew that he had not put sufficient pressure upon Ramon to push him to crisis point. He laughed.

'I'm glad you said fatal, Ramon. Tell her about the banker's wife. Your version should be interesting.'

Ramon frowned at him, but kept his overall control. 'She threw herself at me. It was a dance of some kind. I had to act with good manners but I didn't expect her to act so passionately. She made me a gift of money and begged me to take her away. I refused, and she took her own life, with my knife. It was awful. I cleared out and I only began to forget when I reached Sundown, this chateau, and you.'

Madame la Baronne seemed afraid to react in any way. Her beautiful face was drained of colour. Mike took up the story. 'You got the money, which was your original intention, and when she knew you were abandonin' her, she was on the point of denouncin' you when you pulled your favourite trick! You threw one of your knives, with great accuracy.'

'*Madeleine*, this man is demented. Take no notice of him. Only get rid of him in some way, or, or I shall be moved to violence. I am not so good under this sort of strain. That was why I left *la Legion*.'

Mike cleared his throat. His nerves were also under some strain. 'The cover-up is off. Mr. Charlton Wagner, the banker and widower, is in town with others. It's possible they may have drummed up a vital witness. In any case, only the collection of a federal officer has delayed his arrival so long.' *Lies, Mike thought. Cunning lies.*

With a muted cry of anger, the Frenchman finally made his move. He grabbed *Madame* round the middle and literally carried her over to the antique chest of drawers. His breath was given out in a sigh of relief as his grasping right hand closed over the belt. His gun and knife were back in his possession.

Molly gave a tortured cry and half slumped over the settee. *La Baronne*, a drooping unwilling shield found herself viciously prodded in the back. She stiffened through painful necessity. Mike hovered, his .45 Colt to hand, knowing he could not shoot until Madame was released.

No one interfered as Perrier backed out of the door with his human burden.

Mike moved to Molly, and stretched her out on the settee. Meantime, the near end of the back garden was suddenly ringing with raucous French voices.

16

Ramon was away across the back lawn, moving with a tigerish grace, in spite of the reluctant well-nourished woman he was dragging along.

'*A moi, la Legion! Suivez-moi, avec les chevaux! Vite!*'

Perrier's hoarse, angry orders sounded like a battle rallying cry for the Foreign Legion cavalry. The response came from the stable quarters, where Ribaud and Braun had been anxiously awaiting developments. Now that they knew what was expected of them they moved with the speed of long training.

Mike hurled himself out of the kitchen door and hid behind a low hedge. He guessed where Perrier was heading for, and rapidly shaped his plans.

'Earl! Look out for trouble up there! He's bolted, an' armed! Don't hit *Madame*, who is his prisoner!'

This shouted piece of information had the effect of drawing a short fusillade of bullets from the stables. Mike ducked and rolled and finally came up round the front corner of the building, breathless but unhurt.

'Hey, Johnnie, get that chestnut saddled, *muy pronto*! An' keep well down! I'm comin' over!'

Another bullet chipped the corner of the building as he began his jinxing run across the avenue to where the Indian and the horses were located. Mike dived over the hedge, temporarily lost his Colt, and had to scramble after it. No fewer than six revolvers pumped shells into the pretty fringe decorations round the top of the priest's surrey as the desperate Perrier hurled himself aboard and furiously whipped the startled grey horses into instant action. *Madame* shrieked and clung to one of the canopy supports as if her life depended upon it.

The lightweight vehicle jolted into the avenue and turned north. Ramon was concentrating so hard that he did not have the time to look back. Had he done so, he would have seen his henchmen actually emerging from the side of the house already mounted on their horses, and towing his formidable black stallion on a short lead. They turned north, as well, most of their attention being concentrated in the direction of the burial plot, to the northeast.

A second fusillade of bullets began to pass very close. Riding Indian fashion, they fired back and won a brief respite. Over the other side of the avenue, Two-Feathers had surrendered the chestnut to its owner and busied himself with preparing the other horses for the road.

He clicked his tongue softly as the two mounted men with the led horse appeared in view. Discarding the horse chores, he raised a workmanlike Henry rifle to his shoulder; quietly rose into a standing position. As soon as the 'guards' were sufficiently distracted, he lined up on the tall man, shot him through the head, and turned his attention to the other.

Ribaud reacted swiftly, firing off a Colt left-handed and without looking. This had the effect of making Mike and Two-Feathers duck out of sight. Earl, himself, having run across the lawn to the spot where the surrey had been parked, knocked Ribaud out of the saddle with a careful shot, having held his weapon with both hands.

Mike then mounted up, breathlessly called for Two-Feathers to get his allies mounted and in pursuit. The action was beginning to resolve itself. As he put the chestnut at the fence, he had a vision of old *Monsieur le Comte*'s lined and trusting face when they last met.

The chestnut cleared the fence, but not without trailing its shoes. Mike landed well, turned it towards the north and cleverly dodged a riderless dun horse which threatened to mar his progress. One after another, Earl and the two Bayer brothers appeared in view, breathless, frustrated and perspiration-streaked.

Mike waved to them briefly and gave his horse a series of short jabs with the rowels. It responded. At the same time, an unexpected rifle shot came from the west side of the hedge. Just a few yards behind the rider, Jacques Ribaud flopped in death, deprived of a last telling shot at the Texan by the alertness of the Indian.

Leaving his allies to follow, Mike put all he had into making the chase a short one. Inside three hundred yards, the town came to an end. Tree stands, great patches of scrub and gnarled upthrusts of rock broke up the landscape over a series of undulating hills spreading for several miles.

A faint eddying of dust over the narrow wheel marks indicated the direction which the surrey had taken. Mike supposed that the matched greys were in good fettle, but not necessarily trained to do the work which Perrier was now asking of them.

Clearly, the runaway needed to get himself better mounted than he was. Shaft horses were all right when there were no saddle horses around. As soon as it became clear to Perrier that his stallion and his assistants were out of the reckoning, he would have to seek out some place where he could beg, borrow or steal another horse.

Two things gradually began to trouble Mike. Firstly, he knew by the chestnut's breathing and slightly laboured action that he had made a mistake. It was still tired after its protracted endeavours in the last week or two. He should have used the palomino. Secondly, Mike did not know the land to the north of Sundown particularly well.

Mike's confidence began to ebb. He wondered who would inherit all the Beauclerc possessions if *Madeleine* had the misfortune to lose her life on this tricky occasion. What if Perrier made it away, and held her to ransom? Mike groaned. One after another, brief scenes from the less irksome days he had spent in Beauclerc service went through his mind.

He recollected one occasion when he had driven French visitors to a horse ranch and training establishment a mile or two to the east of north. His memory did not turn up any other habitations in the vicinity.

By this time, he reckoned that the chestnut would not be moving any faster than the twin horses pulling the surrey. He was out of touch with his quarry, and his friends were a long way behind. It was, perhaps, a time to gamble.

From the highest point on a ridge, he spotted the distant ranch through a spyglass. The trail which linked up with it had a lot of winding to do on account of difficult rock formations. He decided to take a chance and cut across the unbroken terrain. A lot depended upon it, and he knew it.

★ ★ ★

The main part of the horse ranch was situated at the far end of the hill-perimetered valley. At the near end were two buildings, an old stable and a Dutch barn. Two working saddle horses were in the stable at the time.

A score of sheep cropped grass in the big meadow near the lower slopes on the west side. The man in the steeple hat and poncho saw the chestnut horse and rider arrive, and the hurried preparations made by the strange rider before the surrey drove up.

The herdsman, a veteran Mexican with a grey beard, walked around the edge of the meadow and slowly came to a decision. He gave the big lean black and white dog specific instructions. It hurried away from him and spooked the tired chestnut out into the open just as the surrey carrying the man and woman came within fifty yards.

The snarling dog did a good job. The man controlling the reins of the surrey was at once alerted. The fair man who had arrived first was just sufficiently distracted by the dog episode to show himself in his prone ambush position on the roof of the Dutch barn.

At once, the driver of the surrey pointed his gun. Four shots, in all, homed on the edge of the wooden roof. One of them removed the would-be ambusher's stetson, which cart-wheeled down the sloping roof and dropped to the ground.

Wrestling with the reins like a charioteer, Perrier swung the surrey first to one side, avoiding the barn and then turned it again to make a circuit of the two buildings. The wheels protested, but the vehicle stayed upright and carried on. Another half a circuit with the man on the roof desperately looking for an opening which did not come.

As soon as the bullets started to fly the herdsman dropped out of sight. The dog, however, was still active. It suddenly hared after the sweating horses and spooked them into making a run up the valley. The woman screamed a warning of sorts, but the noises going up from the surrey and its team drowned her words.

★   ★   ★

On the roof of the barn, Mike could not see up the valley because the stable roof was in the way. He was aware of the surrey getting steadily further away, however, and as soon as he judged it safe he rose to his feet to get a better view. Unfortunately, mounting dust made it difficult to discern the state of affairs between Perrier and Madame. So, for a short while he remained in the same upright position, wondering whether he ought to get down again or wait where he was until help arrived.

A faint whinny might have acted as a warning, but the sound did not register. Mike was moving towards the edge, prior to getting down, when the reaction came. He felt frustrated due to the action of the dog, and was seriously doubting his ability to take on a task of this sort.

The heavy hand gun down below suddenly boomed. Four more bullets ripped their way through the wooden planking, punctuating Mike's footsteps. Suddenly he was off-balance and actually sliding towards the edge. By a miracle, none of the shells hit him. He was not so fortunate when he clawed for the guttering, however, and his grasping hands failed to get a proper grip.

He went over the edge in a somersault, making a half turn in the air and landed on some thinly scattered straw. A shooting pain coincided with the loss of his Winchester, which discharged itself and was lost to him. He was only slightly off-balance when his shoulders hit the ground. Unfortunately, the left side took nearly all the weight and that was the cause of the pain.

Coming to his feet, nevertheless, in a single bound, he launched himself forward for the only sort of near shelter available. Hay bales. They were two high at the front. Mike went over the top head first and found to his surprise that there was a depression in the middle. The bales were stacked in the form of a hollow square. He was on his knees, sucking in breath and bemoaning the loss of his Winchester when the big revolver barked again.

Mike pivoted about and wondered if his luck would hold, in the event that Perrier continued to pump bullets through the packed bales.

'Show yourself! Stand up an' face me, my fine Texan!'

The Frenchman sounded close and confident. Clearly, Mike would be taking a desperate chance if he peered over the top of the bales in an attempt to see his adversary. His thoughts were not too clear on account of the nausea promoted by his hurt shoulder.

Perrier fired again. So as not to be caught napping, Mike fired back, shot for shot. He hoped to have at least one bullet in hand when Perrier had to reload. It was a nightmare, but surely it would pass! Mike did his counting, estimated that Perrier was reloading and decided to take the big risk.

He was just rising from his knees when the knife with the burning brand attached to it sailed through the air and buried itself in a bale just in front of him. For a moment or two, he thought that the swift movement through the air had extinguished it, but he was wrong. The small fire crackled and blossomed in all directions. The issuing smoke made him cough. His eyes watered, he backed off. Back on his knees and taunted by the high-pitched yelling of his tormentor, he knew his life was in the balance.

The smoke was thick and white and acrid. It swirled in his face, and eddied past him. It seemed that his chances were dwindling. He could fire at random, allow himself to be gradually incinerated, or try to break out. He thought Perrier probably hated him sufficiently to pick him off for certain before making a strategic withdrawal.

His senses were slipping. He thought of poor Roxy, receiving the knife in his throat from below. The sudden death of Eleonora Wagner, and the grief of her husband. And he thought he knew what sort of chance he ought to take. He dropped the six-gun which was becoming too heavy to hold, and fumbled out the two daggers.

With one in each hand, and every second more conscious of the growing heat, he rose to his feet and forced himself to look into the smoke which separated him from the buildings. A wayward cloud dissipated and there was Perrier fleetingly revealed with the Winchester to his shoulder, patiently awaiting his chance. But slightly off-target.

Mike threw the first knife by the hilt. Luck was with him. The blade cut the Frenchman's forearm and distracted him. The second blade was held by its pointed tip, and thrown blind. It hit

Perrier heavily in the chest as he tried a snapshot and buried itself up to the hilt.

Mike succumbed to the smoke. A mere few seconds later, the terrified greys, frantically controlled by the woman in black, came hurtling back into the reckoning. In spite of the mushrooming blaze she managed to steer them close enough to dislodge one side of the blazing square in a glancing collision.

She lost her balance and fell to the ground heavily, but the bewildered herdsman was sufficiently close to haul clear the limp figure on her instructions.

★   ★   ★

Mike Liddell gradually became aware of himself and his surroundings as the pain in his shoulder pushed him back to consciousness. The soft paddings around him were not shroud material, but expensive bedding. He was in one of the rooms on the middle floor of the Chateau Beauclerc.

Birds were busy in the garden and occasionally visible through the windows. He groaned, became aware of his weakness and the bandages supporting his shoulder. Faint though his voice was, the door opened and a vision with long swaying copper-coloured tresses ghosted across the floor and stood beside him.

Molly O'Callan looked drawn, and relieved. She mopped the perspiration from his brow and held up his head while he drank some sort of nectar from a thin china cup.

He spluttered a bit. She mopped him up, lovingly replaced his head on the pillow and stepped back a pace. 'The doctor says you'll sleep yourself better, now that the fever has abated. You were shaking and shivering for a while.'

He licked his lips. 'Molly, did he die?'

She placed her hands on her hips, and stared out of the window, into the middle distance. 'Aye, he died. Two days ago. He went the way your friend, Roxy, died. And that poor woman in Middleton. You fixed him with his own knife. The law of Moses, I suppose. The priest wouldn't have approved, but he's gone.'

'What about *Madame*?'

Molly's eyes underwent a subtle change. 'Oh, she's back, all right, an' fitter than you are, in spite of the tumble she took when she drove the horses into the burnin' bales.'

The rearrangement of the bedclothes seemed to release an expensive scent. Mike knew Molly used only perfumed soap. The smell intrigued him. It came from inside the bed. He knew it to be subtle, expensive, and unique. Moreover, only one person had access to it. *Madame*.

'Did you have to put a warmin' pan in the bed when I had the shakes?'

Molly became evasive. 'I don't know. *Madame*, herself, took over nursing duties at the time. I've never known her put the warming pan between the sheets. She thinks it spoils them. Now stop askin' questions, or I'll call her.'

Mike caught her hand. He drew her closer, chuckling as he did so. Molly knelt beside the bed and placed her head on the pillow beside him. Her copper-coloured tresses were still touching his cheek when he slipped off to sleep again with a half-smile on his face.

THE END